Adventures of a Thought Thief   PART I
Heredity and Hierarchy - the beginning

Written by Beverly A. Burchett
Edited by Denise M. Johnson

Copyright 2019

ISBN # 978-0-9903781-7-4

Printed in the United States of America

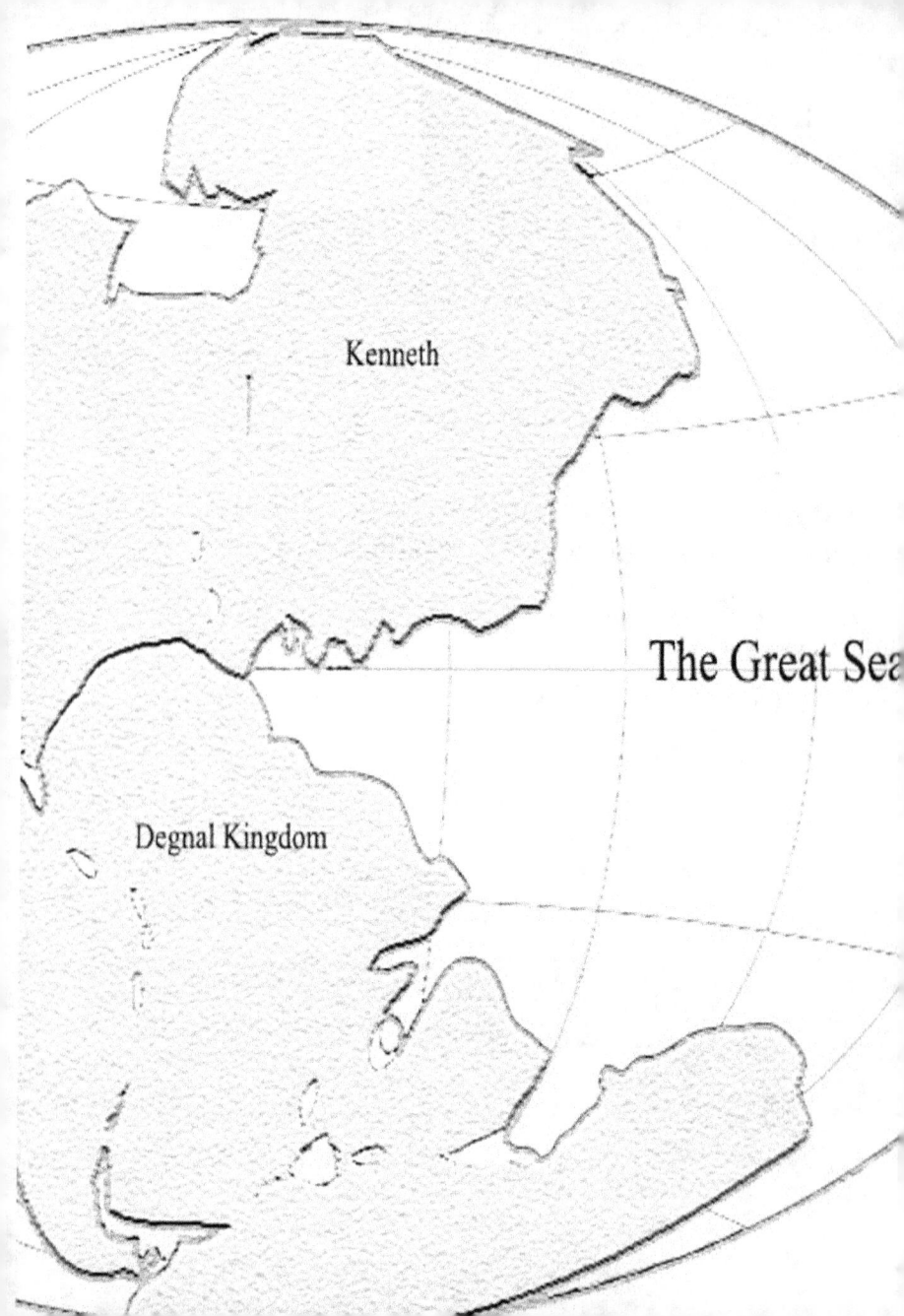

Dedication

To my brothers and sisters who are some of the finest people on earth. They are in my heart and I am the better for it.

Adventures of a Thought Thief

PART I
Heredity and Hierarchy - the beginning

Written by Beverly A. Burchett

CHAPTER 1. He entered the realm of humankind as the Pangaea age was coming to an end. There was still but one massive land mass, called the Great Lands, with lakes, streams and rivers running their way throughout, and one large ocean, called the Great Sea. At this time the earth was undergoing significant transformations in unfathomable ways with each new sun. The world was evolving swiftly as if in labor pains. There were tremors, creating shifts in the earth's crust, with violent eruptions coming from beneath its core. Uncommon beasts roamed freely about its surface. Dramatic climate changes occurred without warning. Typhoons, sand, thunder, torrential rain, snow and hail storms were frequent occurrences. These were traumatic times when just living one's life was a challenge for all of those who walked upon the earth.

He was brought forth on an evening such as described above, filled with black clouds hovering in the skies, releasing an endless assault of frozen hail pelting the ground, a turbulent, gusty, fiery night, the likes of which many had never seen. The winds yowled as if in agony, same as his mother, the Queen, who pushed and pressed with all of her frail might, finally screeching him out of her womb onto the awaiting newly stringed straw mats. He slid forth into a mess so thick that it took nearly a full light for the mid-wives to clean it up. It took another full light for his bronzed tan hue to show through, albeit dotted with splotches of bloody bruises about the head and shoulders, from his body being squeezed on all sides by the narrow hips of his former host. The Queen Mother looked over at him and thought, 'We both look ghastly, but at least I now have a son. Surely, the Sun Maiden has smiled upon me.' She had finally given birth to someone to whom her husband, King Degnal, need not be ashamed.

Asha, the Queen's only daughter, scrunched up her face in disgust at the sight of it, her new brother. Truly, it was the ugliest thing she'd ever seen, and she had the displeasure of witnessing the birthing of mole rats, a spectacle that would forever scar her for life. Yet and still, with that image as a reference, this thing, this presence, she just couldn't fathom. 'Not much to speak of is it?' she gasped to herself, 'To think, we waited nine rounded moons for this?' she sighed. She dared to say that the time spent in anticipation was sorely wasted for such an anticlimactic finale. She wiped the sleep from her eyes, and leaned over the baby basket again to confirm her initial summation. She'd be fair, concluding that she might have rendered her opinion in haste. She would give the dismal creature a second peek.

Unfortunately, upon further investigation, her opinion hadn't changed. She sighed. Alas, it was just as she had briefly surmised. In fact, it was far worse than she thought. The thing had narrow pinched eyes, scaly thin lips pushing their way through its face, and patches of something rough and pasty upon its head. The poor thing didn't even have hair. It was completely bald and the skin color atop its skull was that of an unripe melon. His head looked a little bit like one of the oddly shaped balls in the Degnal Kingdom canons; so small, she felt as if she could fit it in the palm of her hand and crush it. Plus, there was a clear discharge that clumped its way out of the space where the mouth should have been. The same stuff oozed from the dark orbs blinking and staring into space, and out from the nose as well. It looked as if the thing was drooling from every orifice. She held onto the edge of the wooden cradle again and tried her hardest not to stare too closely into its small beady eyes, now staring back up at her. To her, it looked wretched. Asha quickly backed away feeling slightly nauseated; she tried desperately not to vomit.

She made sure not to look at anyone in the room. She was afraid they'd ask her what she thought. Her thoughts were bleak. 'Can we take it back and get another?' she wondered, 'Something more agreeable?' She had seen cute ones before throughout the Degnal Kingdom villages, plenty of them running to and fro. She had even had opportunity to greet a few on occasion. They did not possess the ability of conversing with actual language, of course. They were too young, but she could stomach the way they looked and even showed them regard. She was obligated to do that much; they were her subjects, after all.

However, now that she had seen this one, she realized how mistaken she was to think that all of them would come forth similarly, squishy, and plump. She couldn't believe how naive she was regarding the business of birthing.

This was even worse than the animal they'd just put to rest not four suns ago. And that mangy hound was covered with maggots and fleas and whining incessantly throughout the night. 'There's a thought...' she pondered, '...we should just thrust a blade in it.' After all, that was in fact her job in their realm-deciding whether or not an animal was fit to live. They would be judged by her and if found wanting, slaughtered at her command. This action was then carried out on her sovereign say so.

"Asha!" the Queen Mother called out.

The sound of her mother's voice jarred Asha away from her intense gawking. Though she heard her mother clearly, she turned and faced her slowly. She needed time to pull herself together. She knew better than to show all that she was feeling. She couldn't just reveal her hatred of the wicked, putrid thing outright, especially not to its mother.

"Yes, Queen Mother?" Asha asked in her most well rehearsed, peaceful, obedient tone.

Kena, Asha's handmaiden, raised an eyebrow at witnessing Asha's docile performance. She had often observed this persona of Asha's when she wanted to get something that both Queen Mother and the King had emphatically refused.

"The King and I have already discussed what we shall name him…" she paused, allowing Asha's curiosity to swell, "…Well, would you like to hear it?" Queen Mother asked playfully.

Asha found it hard to keep her composure. She would have rather been stampeded to death by a herd of wild, hungry bison.

"Yes, Queen Mother," Asha managed with mock enthusiasm.

Kena nearly peed from holding in laughter, knowing Asha's true nature to never encompass anything resembling excitement for anyone other than herself.

"We shall call him…" Queen Mother paused, "…ah, on second thought, I shall let the King proclaim it at the naming ceremony."

Asha smiled with tight-lips at her mother the Queen, thinking that she hadn't heard her correctly.

"Did you say his name, Queen Mother?" she asked.

"I did not. Yet, it is a noble name," Queen Mother told her, "You will like it. The name means he who would be king."

Asha shielded her displeasure. She knew that any name for the thing would be uninteresting to her, but to already name him king over her was unconscionable. She also knew that she had to respond warmly to her mother nonetheless.

"Yes, Queen Mother," Asha said as brightly as she could muster.

"Good," Queen Mother said, "Because I'm expecting you to be his closest confidant."

"Queen Mother?" Asha now pouted unable to pretend any longer.

"Asha!" Queen Mother shouted, knowing full well that her willful daughter understood every word.

Asha nodded respectfully to her mother, then asked, "May I go ride now, Queen Mother?"

Queen Mother lifted her eyes and glanced outside of the window. She stayed in that position for several long moments, lost in thought. Not long ago, the sky was pitch black, now the sun was up and the day looked peaceful and calm. Eventually, Queen Mother turned to Asha and held out her arms requesting her to approach. Asha slowly walked across the room and entered into her mother's arms. Queen Mother hugged Asha mechanically.

"Of course," Queen Mother answered, and before she could utter another word, Asha took off for the door.

Then just as Asha was about to exit the room with Kena in tow, Queen Mother cleared her throat, and everyone within earshot stopped what they were doing, turned and listened, including Asha.

"He will need someone as a close friend," Queen Mother said practically in a whisper, "I would like that someone to be you."

Then the Queen Mother glanced over at Asha and nodded once to emphasize that her words were meant as a command. The seriousness of her tone struck a menacing cord with everyone present. Asha lowered her head in obedience then she raised her eyes to meet her mother's steady stare. She knew from her mother's quiet manner that this charge was non-negotiable. Asha slowly nodded back once as a confirmation that she heard and agreed to do what she was told. At that, the Queen Mother was satisfied and turned to face the window again. Then the room grew lively again, immediately with the servants jostling about to attend to the baby and the Queen. Kena unbolted the door for Asha. Then both she and Asha scurried out of the birthing chamber as if escaping.

Asha joyfully ran from the room, leaving the Queen Mother's words locked away safely from her remembrance. Just like that she had forgotten her promise. Suddenly, she had other things on her mind.

She skipped down the long corridors, through the palace racing to see if she could have a word with her father, the King. She was determined to find him and tell him, though she could never tell her mother, that she had decided that they should not keep the new baby after all.

She passed his bed chamber knowing that at this hour he would not be present. She checked anyway, hoping she was wrong. She received no answer when she knocked. If he wasn't in his chamber, he would be holding court.

So, down the steps she went, rounding yet another long corridor until she arrived at the Chamber of Agreement. With the many rooms of the palace, the Chamber of Agreement was the most frequented by the King in the early morning hours. Asha knew that she would find him seated on his royal throne carrying out the business of the day. Some of his subjects, the villagers, would be present and if so, no less than one hundred royal guards would be there as well. Asha was afraid of that last part, because if that were so, she would not be allowed entry.

As she rounded the corner of the corridor to the door of the Chamber of Agreement, royal guards stood rigidly before it. Their weapons were drawn and positioned across the closed entrance. She sighed disapprovingly. She knew that she could not disturb her father, not with the guards standing as if they were at war. She didn't like it. She didn't like it one bit. Especially since she could hear her father's voice in her head saying the same thing to her that he always had.

"Why, they're there to protect the Princess," the King would tell her.

"Am I the Princess, King Father?" Asha would ask.

"Why yes, my daughter, my one and only," he'd reply adoringly.

Asha always liked it when he said such things to her. After all, she was the daughter of the King and she embraced every divine aspect of her privilege. She never had a single day in her life of difficulty. No taxing demands were ever placed upon her. Most of her days were spent in carefree abandon, her nights in comfort and luxury being well feed and on many occasions showered with gifts. Ambitious travelers wishing to impress the King would often bring trinkets and such for her, thinking that if the daughter's heart was warmed so might the King's.

Disappointedly, she stood before the Chamber of Agreement doors contemplating her next move. It only took a few moments of careful reflection to realize that her current mission would have to wait. So, she immediately turned around to find more entertaining amusement, and rushed off head long for the stables, her favorite place. She needed an escape from her awful morning. She could always find gladness in her horse, a jet black stallion named Ox, so called because of his enormous size. She was the only one in the Kingdom allowed to ride him.

She'd be the joyful, happy ten-year-old again, before all this new family addition business took place. She sprinted down the corridors, down the back set of stone steps, through another long corridor, and out the back of the palace to the gravel path that led to the stables. Kena, not far behind, struggled to keep up. Once Asha's face hit the open air, she was back to her old self again.

"I see you're ready to ride, Miss Asha," Delford, the stable boy, said while patting Ox gently on his back, who stood directly beside him.

Asha was elated. Asha was not at all surprised to see her trusty horse harnessed, saddled and ready to go.

Delford always knew when Asha was coming by the sound of her footsteps chomping loudly upon the back concrete hallway of the palace. Without any assistance from Delford, Asha stepped forward and immediately hoisted herself upon Ox.

Kena came rushing out from the palace's back doorway.

"Miss Asha!" she screamed, "Miss Asha..." Kena gasped, out of breath from chasing after her.

Kena couldn't get the words out fast enough of her disapproval in Asha's method of leaping upon Ox.

"...If the King only knew..." Kena screamed in horror, but she was too late.

At this point, all Kena and Delford could do was watch as Asha galloped away from them both down the pathway leading around the palace walls.

As Asha cleared the stables and rounded the gardens, a smattering of the King's guards took off to follow loosely behind her. It was protocol for them to do so. As the King's daughter, she was used to it. She was finally free. She didn't mind the entourage. She was on her blessed horse. She would ride like the wind across the Kingdom lands until her body was sore and darkness descended. Unfortunately, the King's guards would have to keep up pace with her until she tired.

Behind the closed doors of the Chamber of Agreement, was a discussion that would change the course of their peaceable Kingdom, almost as much as the Queen's new arrival had that night. The King and his advisors were assembled to hear urgent news from one of their villages called Kassel. Two of the King's many scouts had the floor. It had come to the scouts' attention that nearly two weeks ago some riders entered this neighboring village. Unfortunately, because they dressed in peasant clothing, these foreigners blended right in. They stayed two nights at a local inn and kept, for the most part, to themselves. A sheep herder, who was occupying the same inn at the time, noticed something poking out of the stranger's cart one night as he was tending his sheep. He looked inside and saw weapons, so, he ran and woke up the inn keeper, who, in turn, ran and told one of the King's scouts.

The scouts waited until the strangers went to sleep that following night, then they crept into the inn's stables and took a peek inside the cart for themselves. They were astonished by what they found. Not only was the cart filled with weapons as the sheep herder had said, but they were not just any kind of weaponry. The weapons they found were those forged in iron unlike Degnal's that were mostly made of clay.

The scouts immediately ran to inform the King's guards who were stationed in the village of Kassel. The guards went straight away to the inn's stable to see all of this for themselves. Upon their investigation, they knew that they had to notify the King at once.

So, accompanied by six of the King's guards, the scouts rode hard for nearly three days to reach Degnal Palace with the news.

"And what was their business there?" the King asked apprehensively.

"They only stayed the two nights, my King, and never spoke to anyone…" Commander Testlar, the Head of the King's guards, said, "…No business was conducted, my King."

"Well, other than their weaponry, can you tell us anything else about them?" the King asked, "What was their tongue?"

"The inn keeper understood them, my King," Testlar answered.

"What did they look like?" the King asked.

"They were exceedingly tall, my King," Testlar answered.

"Exceedingly tall?" an advisor asked, "What is meant by exceedingly tall?"

"Well, my King," Testlar said, "They were at least my height plus a half," replied the guard.

The entire assembly gasped. Testlar was eleven arms' length tall.

"Giants?" an advisor shouted, trying desperately not to show fear.

The King's advisors all broke out into side conversations amongst themselves, each exhibiting varying degrees of panic.

"There's no such thing as giants…" Burton, one of the King's most trusted advisor's, said, "…They must be travelers from the Kenneth territory."

The Kenneth territory was known as being a territory filled with men and women of enormous size.

"These Kenneth territory villagers…" Burton went on to say, "…have never been opposed to the King…" he paused for emphasis, "…I daresay that these men were merely travelers."

Another round of rustling conversation broke out in the room. Even King Degnal looked apprehensive regarding Burton's calm words. He was an astute King, who possessed a healthy share of skepticism and paranoia for all things military.

"Travelers or no," he said sternly, and the room quieted to a hush, "I instruct you to keep a diligent eye upon them," the King demanded Testlar.

"Should we add more guards to the Kassel Village, my King?" asked another advisor.

"Yes," said the King, "Add 1,000 men."

"Yes, my King," Testlar said, "At once, my King."

Testlar immediately bowed, turned on his heels and exited the chamber in order to fulfill King Degnal's command.

Unbeknownst to the King's advisors, King Degnal and Commander Testlar had already spoken in secret about the Kassel Village issue prior to this assembly. Commander Testlar had risen quickly through the ranks of the King's army by his uncanny ability of knowing about things before anyone else. He managed to do so by employing spies throughout the Kingdom. He had them stationed in all the villages of the Degnal Empire and beyond. Routinely, he'd share information that he discovered with the King. Their talks together were never made privy with anyone else, not even with the King's trusted advisors.

During Commander Testlar's clandestine audience with the King, he told the King that his guards had already ascertained the nature of the Kenneth Territory foreigners' visit. Apparently, the two men were conducting trade with one of the Kassel villagers. The Degnal guards ran them both out of the Kassel Village into the wilderness, but not before seizing all their weapons.

Commander Testlar informed the King that Degnal forgers had been employed and had already begun manufacturing iron weaponry, similar to the articles they confiscated. Additionally, enlistment and training of new guards to bolster the King's army had been done as well.

King Degnal was exceedingly pleased by all he heard. He hadn't risen to be King by ignoring possible threats and just sitting idly by waiting for things to happen. He was a man of action, a soldier, like his Commander, Testlar. The King reached in his coffers and handed Commander Testlar all the silver and precious gems he carried, a small fortune for his services. He then gave orders to his Head Chef to prepare a dinner suitable for a King. It was his way of expressing his gratitude to Commander Testlar and his men. He thanked them repeatedly for their quick thinking and ingenuity. That night, Commander Testlar and his men enjoyed being wined and dined by the King's cooks and servers and by the King's special entertainment as well.

When Commander Testlar walked out of the Chamber of Agreement that next day, after having met with the King's advisors, King Degnal felt at ease knowing that the matter of Kassel Village had already been swiftly dealt with. He was no fool. He was shrewd. As King of the Degnal Empire, he'd put on the appearances of being the equitable king with his trusted advisors, a powerful army and loyal subjects. That was the image of a great king. That was a picture of a stable kingdom. No one knew more than he. He also knew the difficulties behind the scenes and the maneuvering that was required in maintaining that perception. He knew that better than anyone.

While King Degnal continued the day's business in the Chamber of Agreement, the nursing chamber commenced their business with the new prince. He was being weighed and measured by the nursing mothers. He received his first royal bath and before their very eyes, his skin became less and less red and his body began to fill out, ever so slightly.

Asha finally returned home from her ride, sweating, tired and hungry. She had only slightly forgotten all about her newly arrived baby brother and she decided that she was not going to think on him anymore that day. Her governess bathed her and prepared her for dinner. That night she would have her supper in her chamber. She would take a walk in the garden. She would play with her dolls and look upon the stars in the night sky. She would be the only child again, if only for a few more evenings. She decided that that was best even if the Queen Mother and her King Father decided to keep the little sniffling, sneezing, and queasy child.

CHAPTER 2. There arose a beautiful sunrise the morning of the Royal Naming Ceremony. Degnal Kingdom was bathed in a bed of pastel hues that sparkled off the royal gardens and filtered through the sun's rays, transforming everything it touched. The Kingdom was all a flutter. The entirety of the Kingdom awoke as if it was a day of harvesting after a severe winter. Regular work would cease and most would be busily occupied in the day's festivities. Practically everyone was employed in some form or fashion assisting with the naming celebration of the new prince. The King's guards looked alert and fine wearing their formal dress uniforms. The village merchants had decorated their shops and filled them to the brim with their best wares. Even peasants were given clean garments to wear and a comfortable area in which to watch the goings on.

The King would suspend all his kingly duties and would spend the greater part of the day in preparation for the ceremony as well. He would be groomed and pampered to perfection, then dressed in his newly tailored royal robes, specifically designed for the occasion. His crown had been cleaned and polished and locked in its cabinet within the Great Hall. A new staff had been carved to include both his daughter Asha upon it, as well as the image of a boy, his son. It had taken several moons to choose a skilled craftsman just for that task, for it wasn't an everyday occurrence for a King to name an heir. In fact, the last time one was named was at Asha's birth. That was ten winters ago. At that time, everyone was well aware of the fact that King Degnal had hoped for a son. He had made mention of it so often, that once Asha was born the naming ceremony was almost called off on account of his disappointment. It was rumored that he carried on with the ritual only to save face. It was grand as well, but by no means as opulent as his son's was shaping up to be. With this one, attention would be given to every detail. Earlier that spring, his Secretary sent out royal invitations to those of nobility throughout the Kingdom and abroad. Well known wealthy families, dignitaries, officials, members of other royal families, and the like were coming from far and wide, all wanting to be a part of the festivities and desiring a glimpse at the person who would eventually be Degnal's new King.

The band had already begun playing music within the palace walls. They played a celebratory song that reflected the character of Degnal. The song was very familiar to everyone, a song that spoke of the Harvest god who, out of his benevolence, gave a barren woman permission to conceive a child. The Harvest god watched as the child grew throughout its life and helped it to succeed. Some believed the god developed a great love for the child and wanted it all to itself. Eventually, the Harvest god created a scenario whereby the mother of the child died, leaving the child alone and abandoned. The Harvest god then stepped into humanity and raised the child himself.

Asha, the Princess, was being readied for this grand occasion too. She wore a fine silk sapphire colored dress that came down just above the ankles. The finishing and trim were made of pure silver. The sheer weight of the garment was designed specifically for her, in order to make her walk steady and sure. She practiced for weeks just to get her gait as perfect as possible. Her father had explicitly instructed her tutors to assist her. With the garment on, she looked precisely the way a little Princess was supposed to, sweet and poised. Yet, beneath the elegant exterior there still lurked the mischievous child. She was actually snickering under her breath. She was hoping that as soon as the villagers and her father laid eyes upon the infant, that no one would believe the child could ever be king. She felt sure that when they took one look, they all would want to do what she had been dying to do since she first saw it - kill it.

She didn't share her dislike of the baby with anyone, not even Kena, whom she trusted with her life. She was smart. Anyone saying anything against the royal family in mixed company would be put to death. It was a Kingdom law. She kept her thoughts to herself. She even kept her head down so no one could discern what she was thinking. She decided that for the remainder of the event she would smile incessantly, really over do it, so that no one would be the wiser of what she truly felt.

The nursing mothers had begun their morning by bathing the royal prince, clothing him and preparing him for his first royal visit with his father, King Degnal. The King had not set eyes upon the baby boy yet. It was customary in Degnal to wait a full moon if not longer for a new heir to be presented before a King. Traditionally, it was believed to be bad luck to present a baby before a King who could barely sit up. Even at an early age, the new heir was required to show signs of strength and power, and none of the inklings of weakness. Once the baby was able to demonstrate its royal capabilities, the new heir would then officially be Christened and named by the King. The Queen would have very little to do with the child after that. Her job had already been accomplished. She bore it and assisted in its delivery. It was then up to the King to facilitate its growth and development. The Degnal Kingdom's lineage consisted of Kings rearing Kings. It was looked upon as abhorrent for a Queen to assume these duties. In the minds of the Degnal Kingdom, Kingdom business was better suited for the King. Therefore, King Degnal was responsible for the boy's training, as he was destined to be the next Degnal King.

The palace began to fill with the King's invited guests. The guests presented their royal invitations and then joyfully stepped inside. Those who had traveled from afar were led into a wing of the palace for out-of-town guests. They had arrived carrying luggage and would be given a chamber to sleep in for the remainder of the ceremony, while, local guests were escorted directly into the Great Hall. All the guests possessed gifts of the finest of jewelry and tapestries, fine arts or articles of silver to be added to the royal treasury. The Naming Ceremony was one of the most important ceremonies in the Kingdom. The most elite families of the Kingdom would be represented among the guests. It was a time of lavish food, the King's best wine and days upon days of spectacular entertainment. Princess Asha's birth was honored in celebration for fourteen days. Apart from royal weddings and the royal parties for the night lights and the festivals for morning lights, there was nothing more distinguished in the Kingdom than the landmark moments of the royal heirs.

The Royal Baker had been in preparation of the menu for half the year. The five course dinner would start with lamb kabobs, caramelized hardboiled eggs, a choice of barley or lentil soup, an entrée of supple roasted ham, oxtail stew, tender pork, wild duck, and Peri Peri chicken with farmed millet, a slow cooker root vegetable Tagine, and a potato casserole, then to finish, some the most delectable baked treats for dessert, including the King's favorite bricks of sweet fudge. The Royal Baker had employed some two-thousand strong cooks, bakers and servers to assist in the royal kitchen. Additionally, all meals were to be served to the guests on the royal china, with the royal silverware.

Even the napkins were especially made for the occasion by the royal seamstresses. It would be the banquet to rival all banquets. The singers, musicians, dancers, jugglers and magicians were auditioned and rehearsed to include only the finest of the arts. All of this was being done in honor of the King's first son.

Although, only those from the King's exclusive invitation list were allowed inside the palace, all the Degnal villagers, those within the court walls and those afar would enjoy the festivities. Musicians were commissioned to play music in all public areas in and around the vast kingdom. Additionally, food tables were set up in public places for the purpose of serving those outside the courts. The entire kingdom would have a share of the King's wine. One glass per person would be served in village bars. King Degnal enjoyed the idea of everyone toasting the arrival of his new heir.

The King spared no expense, especially after the many years that he and the Queen Mother had suffered in one disappointment after another. The Queen Mother miscarried twice and endured three still births. Throughout their struggles, of course, Asha was continually being groomed to become heir to the throne. Until very recently, that is. She was taught all about weaponry; how to sword fight, throw a spear, and to hunt. She learned several languages and also how to read and write. She was accomplished in every way in her role to assume the throne, however, as a female child, she would endure countless hardships from the male dominated world she would rule. She was told repeatedly to always be on her best behavior in order to sway them towards her success in this role.

The Queen Mother emerged from her dressing chamber looking wholly replenished. She was dressed in an indigo and honey colored, hand-spun, lacewing silk gown. It cascaded sweepingly down her handsome body to the floor with a five arm length train. Two servants had to follow behind to hold it up. When she walked, it appeared as if she were floating on air. She was elegant, statuesque and beautiful. She met her husband, King Degnal, outside the double-doors that led into the Great Hall.

Inside the Great Hall, a single kudu antelope horn sounded and out stepped the Royal Announcer into the center of the room.

"Ladies and gentlemen, please welcome your King

and Queen," he proclaimed to a hushed crowd.

The King and Queen then stepped elegantly into the Great Hall followed by their servants and their armed guards. Their hands were clasped together as they glided toward their thornes located at the front of the hall. As they traversed the room, their royal subjects knelt in honor of their presence. Only once they were seated, did the music play and the celebration officially begin. Moments later, Princess Asha entered the hall, but through the back entrance, followed closely behind by Kena. She took her seat without fanfare, and without recognition on the part of the guests. She preferred being able to slip in and out unobserved. She was required to stay for dinner and the announcement of the baby. She had just arrived and was already looking forward to being allowed to exit for the night. She only wanted to stay long enough to see everyone's reaction to the horrifying sight of her new brother. She would stay and endure in anticipation of their disapproval.

Seven hours into the festivities, the kudu horn sounded again and the Royal Announcer once again stepped into the center of the Great Hall.

"My King, my Queen, Ladies and Gentlemen, please welcome his royal highness, the Prince," he proclaimed.

All eyes were immediately drawn to the back of the hall. The double doors swung open and the Prince's Governess walked in accompanied by two armed guards. In her arms, she carried the Prince. The spectators stopped what they were doing and stepped aside for her to walk down the center of the room to the King and Queen. Everyone tried their best to get a look at the Prince. The Governess had him covered from head to toe in a white cotton cloth.

Asha rose to her feet as did some of the other guests seated at the royal table. She wanted to observe everyone's reaction. She was appalled when she saw them smiling and giggling. Some even saluted and waved at him. She was initially disappointed until she realized that they couldn't yet see him. She sat back down, feeling sickened by the guests' deliberate act of pretending before the King. She looked upon her father. She knew that her father was discerning enough to know that some of these citizens among him could not be trusted. She would have to wait for him to give his final word on the matter.

The Governess approached the throne. She knelt

before the King and Queen respectfully. Then she unwrapped the little baby, fully uncovering him from the fabric above and beneath his body.

"You may rise," the King ordered her.

As the Governess rose, she stretched out her arms and extended them forward displaying the baby before the King and the Queen. King Degnal and Queen Mother also rose, and stepped forward to gaze upon the newborn baby. While King Degnal plunged ahead toward the infant, the Queen hesitated and stealthily held her breath. She knew that the baby would be acceptable to her husband the King, of that she was sure. However, in light of what she saw during the birth night, coupled with all her pregnancy troubles, she was suddenly less sure. Like all mothers, she hoped for the best for her children. 'What if something is wrong with the child?' she thought. She had done all she could. If she had to do all of this again, she knew that it would surely kill her. She hoped beyond measure that her husband, the King, would look past what she saw on that dreadful, awful night that the baby was born, and see something noble in his son.

From where he was standing, the King couldn't see the baby clearly. He needed to get closer, so, he took a step down from the platform, reached into the cloth covering the baby and scooped him right out of the Governess' arms. Then King Degnal looked at his son for the first time. He didn't know what to expect, but he was still surprised by what he saw. The Queen Mother nearly collapsed from holding in her breath. She dizzily backed up and sat back down as gracefully as she could upon her throne. Asha glanced over at her mother curiously. Then she quickly went back to observing her father. She needed to see what the King thought. The King's back was to her, so she then relied on the reactions of the spectators in the hall. All of their eyes were glued to the King and to his new heir.

King Degnal took an unusually lengthy amount of time examining his son. He gazed upon him as if they were the only two people in the room, the world. At first, all he noticed was the baby's smile; that smile he would know anywhere, for it was his own. Then the King looked into the baby's eyes. Those eyes were familiar too; those were the eyes of his dearly departed mother. They were a beautiful hazel color, that sparkled even when light was not upon them. The baby's skin was tan, like his own and as smooth as rosewood and even all over. The King then reached into the cotton cloth and picked up the baby from underneath. One hand was gently supporting the baby's newly formed head and the other was placed beneath his knees. The King held his son up and displayed him to the crowd.

"Honored guests, please welcome…" the King's eyes swelled with tears, "…my son, Prince Oban Degnal," the King shouted.

Loud, raucous applause and cheers of congratulations broke out in the hall. The band immediately began playing again. They changed their tone from the upbeat lighthearted song selection that played during dinner to Degnal Kingdom's celebrated anthem about the Harvest god.

CHAPTER 3. Kena painstakingly cracked her eyes open after only three hours of sleep. She had to peel herself from her cot and splash water on her face in order to shake off her tiredness. As the Princess' first lady, it never mattered how she was feeling, which was deliriously exhausted. It wasn't even dawn, yet she was up and had already begun the preparations for the Princess' daily activities. She placed the kettles on the hot coals and while waiting for them to heat up, pulled out several articles of clothing for the Princess to wear that day. The Princess would need at least three to four outfits at the ready whether she wore them all or not. Kena laid them out in the Princess' dressing chamber, then went to start Asha's bath. Now that the palace had emptied of the King's guests, the naming festivities behind them, Kena looked forward to having an ordinary day.

Kena scurried down the corridor to Asha's bed chamber. As much as she enjoyed the lavish food, drink and the enchanting music of the naming ceremonies, thoughts of having a simplified life again lifted her spirits and infused her with glee. Asha was never a moment's trouble for her for as long as she had been in the King's employ. Sure, Asha was mischievous, but until very recently, she was being groomed to be the next ruling member of the Kingdom. Kena had a coveted job. Her only requirements were to keep track of the King's daughter and to make sure that she made all the appointments on her daily agenda. Most mornings Asha took her breakfast in her bed chamber. Next came her lessons in the library for several hours. Afterwards, she would have a meal in one of the many palace dining halls, occasionally with the Queen Mother. The remainder of her day would be spent in the gardens, or in and around the stables, in the game room, that was Kena's favorite place, or they would enjoy long walks throughout the sprawling Kingdom territory.

Kena didn't initially think much in seeing Asha's bed chamber door ajar. She pushed through and stepped across the threshold.

"Asha, dear," she called out.

Asha didn't answer straight away. Nothing usual there. Asha often preferred to remain in bed while Kena conducted her standard routine of gently stirring the Princess awake. Kena walked over to the window and tied up the enormous velvet drapes that hung on both sides. A rush of warm sunlight flooded the chamber. Kena smiled as she looked out on a spectacular view of Degnal Kingdom. From that vantage point, it was absolutely breathtaking. The sheer magnitude of the territory always managed to overwhelm her. She could see the mountainous country side in the distance, with its peaks sneaking through thick white ethereal clouds. The plains, moist with dew, made the meadows look like they were filled with stars from the heavenly sky. Kena stole away a moment of joy in what she saw, then she turned to attend to the business of taking care of her charge, Princess Asha.

"Miss Asha…" she called out again, "…It's time to start our day."

After pouring Asha a glass of water and placing a wedge of lemon in it, she went to gently nudge her awake.

Kena approached the bedside, dropped the glass upon the floor and screamed. Asha's bed was covered in blood.

Two of the King's guards burst through Asha's chamber doors having heard Kena's shrieks. They immediately stepped around her frozen body and looked upon Asha's bed.

"Where is the Princess?" one guard barked.

Kena had lost all powers of speech. The only thing she could manage was a wooden, stiff-neck turn towards the guard.

"Woman!" shouted the other guard, "Where is the Princess?" he asked.

Kena lowered her head and hunched her shoulders. She felt sick to her stomach. A steady gush of tears began to stream down her face and she actually shook from fear. She was devastated, for she immediately believed Asha was dead and that thought literally paralyzed her. Asha meant everything to her, more to her than anyone else in the world. She had known her since she was born. In fact, they had grown up together. They knew everything about each other, all the other's secrets. Kena was regarded as so much more than a servant. Unfortunately, those thoughts were accompanied by thoughts of what the King would do to her at the disappearance of his daughter. Though there were guards in charge of the Princess' safety, who shadowed her daily movements and were stationed outside her bed chamber at all times, Kena felt certain that they'd somehow manage to convince the King she was responsible. Now with her life in danger and the Princess' life cut short, Kena's wish for a normal day had vanished forever.

Escorted by ten of the King's armed guards, Kena entered a part of the palace that she had never seen, the War Chamber. She'd only heard rumors of what transpired within, and therefore resigned herself to an abysmal fate. Servants had often mentioned in secret of having to scrub blood stains from its floors. It was the only room in the palace where women were not allowed, not even to serve its occupants. King Degnal and his men spent countless days inside of this chamber on one taxing dilemma after another. Asha confided in Kena once that everything about the room frightened her.

Kena was shoved in. She tripped over her own feet and fell forward onto the ground. She was scared out of her wits. Her heart raced through her chest. Her hands shook. Her knees were so weak, she could barely stand. She struggled awkwardly to get back up. Before she could manage that, someone snatched her from behind and pulled her to her feet. She didn't see who it was, but out of the corner of her eye, she saw Commander Testlar walking away from her and back to his post beside King Degnal.

Now that she was upright, she took that opportunity to peruse the room. It was an enormous circular hall with thick clay walls. Approximately, eleven arm lengths above the floor were windows that wrapped around three quarters of the room's top. Tables were lined in several semi-circles and at each sat either a King's advisor, or a Head of State, or some other high ranking serviceman from the King's Army. It was then that Kena realized that she was led into the very center of it all. She felt so utterly sick to her stomach and helpless.

"Kena, where is my daughter?" the King asked solemnly.

"I…" Kena started and stopped.

Her throat was suddenly too dry for her to speak.

"…I…" Kena tried again.

King Degnal glanced over at Commander Testlar. Testlar stepped forward.

"Miss, we need to act on this as quickly as possible…" Testlar said, walking closer to Kena, "…Your help is vital. What happened this morning?"

Kena broke into tears.

"Miss, now!" Testlar said sternly, "The Princess' life is at stake!"

"Sir...I...I do not know what happened this morning..." Kena said, "...I entered the chamber. I ran the bath. I tied the drapes..." she sobbed, "...then I turned and...I saw..."

Kena sunk to the floor and sobbed uncontrollably.

"Where were the guards?" Advisor Butler shouted out to no one in particular.

Commander Testlar pointed to the two of his guards who were stationed at the Princess' chamber door. The guards immediately marched forward and into the center of the room. Kena remained hunched over weeping.

"Tell us what happened last night," demanded Commander Testlar to his guards.

"Commander, we escorted Princess Asha to her bed chamber before the dawn's light. She was accompanied by her ladies, six in all. Approximately two hours later, all but one left the chamber, Commander," a guard reported.

"Who was left in the chamber with the Princess?" the King asked.

"My King, the one who reads to her," the guard told him.

"Have you accounted for the whereabouts of all the ladies?" the King asked.

"My King, we have, only…" Commander Testlar replied.

"Only what?" asked the King.

"Only, the storyteller has gone missing too, my King," Commander Testlar said.

The room fell silent. Only the whimpering of Kena could be heard as the men in the War Chamber contemplated a rather grim reality. Commander Testlar broke the silence.

"My King, we must assume that one of the guests stole away with the Princess," Advisor Butler suggested.

"My thoughts exactly," said the King regrettably.

He sighed at the thought of having one of his invited guests do such a thing to him. He was more than unnerved. He was bitterly angry.

"I demand that she be found at once!" he shouted.

"My King," replied Commander Testlar.

"I want the entire empire searched! Leave nothing unexamined! Every home, every stable, every tree in the forest!" shouted the King.

"My King," replied Commander Testlar.

"And as for the Princess' ladies, throw them all in prison!" shouted the King, "Perhaps then they will know something about my daughter's whereabouts, with only millet and water to eat!"

Commander Testlar merely nodded to two of his guards, and they immediately lifted Kena up and dragged her out of the War Chamber.

CHAPTER 4. On account of Princess Asha's disappearance, war had broken out between King Degnal and all of his subjects. The following three winters were said to be the most turbulent times in Degnal Kingdom history. Gone seemingly forever was the King who sent musicians forth to play throughout the lands, the benevolent King who wanted all of his subjects to partake in a toast of his best wine at the Naming Ceremony of his son. The lavish food, the entertainment and the merriment that lasted twenty straight suns were a distant memory on the minds of his people.

Now, the King's army thundered into every single village and forcefully ransacked all of its domiciles. Nothing was secure from their destructive hands. His men tore through homes with battering rams reserved for war. They even lifted the roofs off of most in order to make sure the Princess wasn't hidden within. Barns and shacks were searched and then burned down to the ground in a fury. Men, women and children alike were brought in for questioning and if found in any way to be suspicious, were then arrested, tortured and then sent to prison. The King's builders had to erect additional structures to house the amount of people brought in by the guards. Some villages were almost completely cleared out of men, for the arrests.

The King's anger could not be satiated. He was so overwhelmed with grief that he actually rode with the army into the Degnal villages. Areas would be surrounded by armed guards and all subjects were forbidden to leave until a thorough hunt for the Princess was conducted. He'd then oversee every inquisition, trial, and torturing held in that village. He even demanded daily progress reports on inquiries conducted in other villages. Guards had to ride throughout the night in order to keep up with the King's unnerving requests for moment by moment information.

It was an extremely dark time for the Degnalites. No one was safe from the King's wrath. Even his advisors were scrutinized by the King's guards, especially Advisor Burton, who would often boldly voice his opinions while they were in session.

"How dare you search my chamber!" shouted Advisor Burton, as the guards rummaged through his belongings back at the palace.

"Does the King know that you are conducting this search?" he asked.

The guards went about their business without answering the Advisor. At the King's specific orders, they were to make random investigations throughout the year. They didn't have to answer to the advisors. Their orders were to only speak to the King or their Commander. The King desired to catch his advisors unaware, hoping to discover some slip-up of foul play. This method of randomly searching the palace went on as long as the King was away in his other territories. Even the Queen Mother was not exempt from these intrusions. However, she handled them with a bit more grace.

"How goes it?" she asked the two guards one evening who stormed into her bed chamber in the middle of the night.

She was abed in her dressing gown. A single candle lamp light shone in her room where she could just make out the pesky guards' faces. They tried not to let it show, but the guards were startled to see her awake and that she appeared to have been waiting up for them. The vigor the guards exuded upon their arrival suddenly fell flat. They then conducted a lackluster perusal of the room. Not a single article was tossed about, but carefully picked up and equally placed neatly back in place. Afterwards they respectfully backed up out of the chamber quickly and quietly.

The Queen knew her husband, the King, well. He was fiercely territorial of everything he possessed, and among those possessions he coveted, one of them was her. That very next morning, she sent word through a trusted rider to her husband. The note spoke in detail about the guards who trespassed into her bed chamber. By nightfall, the guards were released of their duties. A set of replacement guards were employed in their stead.

The random searching did not cease, but the Queen was never awoken in the middle of the night again. Instead, the guards would wait until the Queen was out for her daily walk about the gardens or out visiting with Prince Oban, before they'd enter her chamber. Otherwise, the Queen was like everyone else in the Degnal Kingdom, in a kind of prison one way or the other.

Unfortunately, while the Kingdom was in the throes of their endless search for Princess Asha, sadly nothing was being done for the upkeep of their precious domain. Try as they might to farm or to tend to their animals, villagers were constantly being called upon to service the King's vast army instead. Each village was in essence hosting thousands upon thousands of troops, tending to all of their daily requirements and neglecting their own. With the widespread panic, torching of property and general lack of maintenance of the lands, things began to fall sharply into disrepair. Thriving villages quickly began to look like wastelands. The future of the Degnal territories was looking bleak.

The amount of distrust, suspicion and sheer fear kept the villagers from ever voicing their concerns. At that time, giving one's opinion was dangerous throughout the Degnal Kingdom. Even the King's advisors were remiss to speak out on behalf of the empire's interests in disagreement of their King. Unfortunately, the reality was such that there wasn't a single individual who wasn't being harassed by the King's guards in some fashion or another. King Degnal was blinded emotionally and simply couldn't see that the Degnal Kingdom was on the verge of collapse.

Meanwhile, in a land on the other side of the world from the Degnal Kingdom, across the great Tethys sea, sat another King who, among other talents, was quite adept himself of knowing things that others would have preferred him not to know. Like King Degnal, he had an insatiable appetite for obtaining information; gathered mostly surreptitiously through his elaborate network of elite spies. They were everywhere, not just in and around his vast Kingdom, but in all surrounding territories as well. Far and wide, these spies were enlisted and paid handsomely for one reason and one reason alone, to listen. They would then bring back every single morsel, every juicy tidbit, or thread of news to the king, namely secrets. King Runmari prided himself on being very well informed and would give rewards to those agents who went above and beyond in this calling.

Some of the things King Runmari learned were used socially, making him appear to be a man of the world, but a far greater portion was utilized politically. Like his father before him, King Runmari knew the value of knowing the goings on in his Kingdom and those elsewhere. In his short five year reign, the Runmari Kingdom, a territory he acquired after his father's untimely death by assassination, the Kingdom grew at an unprecedented rate. This was largely due to King Runmari spending the greater part of his rulership expanding it. His acquisitions encompassed twenty-five additional kingdoms; kingdoms that he had conquered easily by exploiting knowledge of his opponent's weaknesses.

He'd visit these territories under the guise of traveling as a royal diplomatic convoy sent to create alliances, bringing with him expensive jewels, fabrics, and spices as gifts to show his sincerity. Most of his victims were unaware of his true intent and would allow him entry into their palaces, happily displaying their wealth, and unfortunately their vulnerabilities as well. All the while, King Runmari's troops would lay in hiding, waiting for his signal to seize these lands by brute force if necessary, killing off anyone who stood in their way. King Runmari's men were brutal and unrelenting, all relishing in their king's taste for blood and for acquiring possessions. Some of his troops had just recently come across two men from Kenneth. Just for sport, they mercilessly beat them in order to obtain information for their King. When the foreigners refused to give them any, King Runmari's troops then gouged out their eyes and cut out their tongues.

That next morning, King Runmari blissfully awoke, literally drooling over his next intended conquest. The kingdom he now had in his sights was Degnal Kingdom. He dreamt of climbing upon its snow capped mountains and enjoying a dip in its cool streams, riding upon its plush meadows, marveling at its majestic fields. He was told that its farmlands were lush and plentiful, its inhabitants strong and able. King Runmari looked forward to governing them and ruling over them. This would be the *jewel* of his treasury, Degnal Kingdom being larger in size than half his other kingdoms combined. He was still basking in the pleasure he felt upon hearing about the current state of Degnal.

Many suns ago, he had convened with some of his spies for his routine royal update. To his delight, they had returned from their travels with some intriguing news. As usual, King Runmari received the news seated stoically without expression. As he listened, though he'd never let it show to them, he was all a flutter as they spoke. He savored the secrets of others, while remaining tight-lipped about his own.

"It's empty, my Lord," one soldier spy told the King.

"Empty?" King Runmari asked causally, "How so, empty?"

King Runmari sat on his throne while his royal barber trimmed his beard. The barber was panic-stricken.

The last twelve barbers had their throats cut for accidently nicking the King's face. For this reason, the barber wore a rope tied around his waist. If he offended the King, he'd be slashed and his dead body would be dragged out from the chamber. The barber's hands literally shook as he carried on with his business. Unfortunately, he couldn't distinguish between the King's rough, charcoal skin and his prickly, matted, black whiskers. He was forbidden to ask his King to sit still. He had to instead predict every abrupt jerk forward or back the King might make. This was dangerous employment, but if executed well, they were paid handsomely and the job could last a lifetime. The only saving grace for the barber trade was the fact that King Runmari wore his hairs long and scruffy in times of war, and their King took great pleasure in being at war.

"Yes, my Lord. King Degnal is a three sun's ride from his palace," said another soldier.

King Runmari licked his dark, thick cracked lips and gave no reaction to the news. He didn't wish for anyone to know his inner thoughts on the matter, though, his head swelled with visions of grandeur at snatching up such an enormous kingdom with its considerable riches. Having Degnal Kingdom would make him ruler over much of the immense Great Lands, giving him ports along the entire eastern side of half the world. He was practically giddy with enthusiasm at the notion of such a prize. His father before him wouldn't have dreamed of such a massive capture. In the history of their kingdom, no other king had done more than he had at expanding their territory. King Runmari took a deep breath and quieted his thoughts. He would hold in his excitement and continue his probe.

"And why is King Degnal so otherwise preoccupied?" King Runmari asked feigning disinterest with all he was hearing.

He was a shrewd man. He needed to make sure that he would not be charging into a trap. He was always conscious of the idea that even his trusted agents could have dual purposes. That is why he would conduct several of these clandestine meetings throughout the new moon and hear from his other sources as well on this very same issue.

"The Princess Asha has been stolen away, my Lord" a soldier informed him.

"Yes, I am aware of that," King Runmari said nonchalantly as if the soldier was referring to ancient news, "…And?"

"My Lord…" said the soldier perplexed.

The other soldier jumped in with the answer he knew the King wanted to hear.

"My Lord…King Degnal and his guards are away looking into her whereabouts…" the soldier replied with a confused expression.

King Runmari waved his hand abruptly, thereby dismissing everyone except his barber. Not only did King Runmari know where King Degnal and his guards were, he knew what they were up to that very day.

On that sad day for the Degnal villagers, King Degnal and his guards were torturing a group of men who they believed knew more than they were telling about the abduction of the Princess. King Runmari knew this because he helped orchestrate their arrest. His spies were told to go about the villages and spread some carefully worded lies. King Runmari knew that in the state King Degnal was in, rumors wouldn't take long to spread. The spies were to simply ask a very innocent question. They were to inquire amongst the King's guards about a group of men who they claimed were acting suspiciously. In reality, the men in question neither looked suspicious, nor knew anything about the Princess whereabouts. That did not, unfortunately, stop King Degnal from bringing them in, charging them with crimes against their King, and then torturing them within an inch of their lives.

CHAPTER 5. King Runmari arrived at Degnal palace three full moons after he first heard of King Degnal's absence. Unlike his other conquests, he did not travel this time with a large delegation of troops. He didn't have any hiding along the country side either, or waiting in the mountains for a special attack signal. Instead, he and just a handful of his best men ventured forth carrying several wagons full of gifts designed especially for King Degnal. He knew that King Degnal loved silver, so he had the best he could carry in several hundred crates.

If it were any other time, King Runmari would have been required to send a messenger in advance carrying a letter with his royal seal affixed upon it, requesting an audience with King Degnal. He would have had to then await a response, usually accompanied with a royal invitation. King Runmari smiled to himself. There was currently no need for that. As he approached, no one even stopped him to inquire of his purposes there. Normally, there would have been armed guards stationed at every entry point on horseback and on foot. Now the posts were either vacant of guards, else the ones on duty were slack and undisciplined. King Runmari couldn't believe the vulnerabilities of Degnal Palace.

King Runmari was well aware of the fact that he could have easily just taken the kingdom by force, of that he was certain. It wasn't even in question. 'But why risk it?' King Runmari thought. He didn't like the possibility of King Degnal's men returning unexpected. In his mind, they'd come scurrying back angry and now prepared for battle. No, King Runmari wanted his victims to be unaware. He preferred to have everyone already home, nestled in their beds. That way he could surround them all, including their King, as they slept.

The Degnal Palace tower guards did see King Runmari approaching from afar and sent King Degnal's messengers to alert the palace guards of his arrival. They knew who it was by his royal colors of black and gray distinguishing him from any other king.

"How many men?" Advisor Burton asked the messenger.

"Twenty in all," the messenger replied.

"Small…" Advisor Burton mouthed slowly, thinking that the Kingdom should be safe with so few troops coming to visit.

Advisor Burton didn't want to suspect foul play though he was naturally apprehensive. He wanted to take comfort in this surprise visit but there were only three-hundred Degnal guards in and around the palace. He knew that with so few guards at hand, they wouldn't be able to defend themselves adequately against a large army attack. Nonetheless, he had to show strength.

"We will see them in the Autumn Hall," Advisor Burton informed the messenger with a voice that quivered as he spoke.

The royal messenger ran off to relay this information to the other royal advisors, who in turn, all readied themselves for the visitor. The royal guards were already told and stood at attention at each of their posts. Everyone took this foreign King's visit as an intrusion and readied themselves. They were sworn to represent King Degnal and protect the Kingdom at all times and would do so accordingly.

Typically, the Queen Mother was called on for these occasions of welcoming dignitaries while the King was away, but she had secluded herself from all rituals ever since her daughter disappeared.   She hadn't even been notified that the palace was receiving a guest.

Once King Runmari entered the palace, he was escorted into the Autumn Hall where refreshments were served to him and his men. King Degnal's advisors were already there to greet him. It had been five winters since Degnal palace had received guests. That was the length of time that their King Degnal had been away, searching for his long lost daughter, Princess Asha.

"Welcome, King Runmari," Advisor Burton said, ushering King Runmari and four other men accompanying him into the hall.

Advisor Burton could tell that one of King Runmari's men was his royal taster. He would sample any food served to his King. Another appeared to be King Runmari's messenger and the others were definitely troops. They wore King Runmari's colors under chained armor and carried weaponry upon them.

A server poured wine into a goblet for King Runmari and his royal taster immediately took a sip. The taster continued to stand erect after swallowing the wine.

Moments passed and King Runmari observed that his taster did not kneel over or writhe in agony. Only then did King Runmari taste of the wine himself. Once he drank and swallowed then all others were served from the same pitcher. King Degnal's advisors sighed with relief as King Runmari smiled and nodded in approval of the wine. Advisor Burton had requested in advance that the palace kitchen bring up the best they have from the royal cellar.

"King Runmari, I'm Advisor Burton and these are my fellow kinsmen of King Degnal's royal advisory," Advisor Burton said introducing himself.

King Runmari gestured a greeting to them all.

"A pleasure to meet you all," King Runmari said nodding to each individually, raising his glass in honor of them.

King Runmari pointed to the grapes before him and his royal taster reached forth and popped a few into his mouth. Only after observing no change in his taster's continence did King Runmari taste of the grapes himself. Each food item before him was tasted in a similar manner. With each approval King Runmari gave for the meal, King Degnal's advisors felt more at ease, because they started this meeting feeling tense and unsure of their visitor's motives.

"I come bearing gifts," King Runmari told them.

Then he clapped his hands and the doors of the Autumn Hall opened. At the doorway appeared men carrying trunks of silver trinkets, scarves and other fine fabrics and spices. King Degnal's advisors were impressed with the sheer magnitude of the gifts. The Autumn Hall wasn't big enough to contain them all and some were left outside in the corridors.

"You are most generous and kind," marveled Advisor Burton.

Then Advisor Burton clapped his hands and the royal band began to play music for the assembly.

"Wonderful!" exclaimed King Runmari, expressing his appreciation of the music.

Once the band began to play, the entire room took on a more festive tone and everyone relaxed and ate joyfully. There were even moments when the Degnal advisors reminisced of times gone by when Degnal Kingdom was in celebration and at peace. Advisor Burton leaned over to King Runmari.

"And what brings the King here to our humble kingdom?" Advisor Burton asked.

He didn't wish to appear as if he was in any way

suspicious of this visit, so he put on an air of casual banter between men of the world. King Runmari returned his answer with the same pleasant tone.

"To see the King's son, of course..." King Runmari replied, "...He must be approaching three winters now..." he said as if he were trying to figure out the boy's age.

Truly, King Runmari knew the King's son's age to the minute. He also knew that he already spoke three languages and could play the drums and the flute.

"Five winters to be exact," Advisor Burton gently corrected the King.

"I am traveling forth en route of the Concordia Kingdom to develop trade and have ventured here purely out of respect for your King, King Degnal," King Runmari said in his most reassuring manner.

At that, Advisor Burton leaned over to his messenger and whispered something into his ear. The messenger immediately exited the Autumn Hall. A few minutes later, the messenger returned with six armed guards. The guards stood at the entrance and awaited word from Advisor Burton. Advisor Burton simply nodded to him.

Immediately afterward, the band ceased their music playing and everyone watched as the royal announcer came forth into the Autumn Hall.

"Ladies and gentlemen, his royal highness, Prince Oban," he proclaimed.

Then out from behind the armed guards marched Prince Oban followed by his tutors, his royal steward and nursemaids.

Prince Oban entered the hall looking like the quintessential picture of nobility. He wore a velvet robe of lush green color and a crown atop his angular well shaped head. He had a pleasant expression upon his face but it was by no means a smile, nor a frown. He stood among his servants austerely, looking far more mature than others his age. Gone were any traces of his birth bruises and discolorations. He was handsome. He was in perfect health, with smooth tan skin, sparkling hazel eyes housing remarkable intelligence within.

He greeted his father's advisors with just the slightest movement. He blinked his eyes slowly. The entire hall rose to their feet and bowed before him. Even King Runmari stood and lowered his head in submission, surprised at the amount of authority the little Prince possessed. Despite himself, King Runmari found himself impressed. He had assumed to find a child prince desiring the constant attention and amusement of his wards, prancing around spoiled and fidgety. However, that was not the case with young Prince Oban. He clearly had a handle on his surroundings and seemed quite capable of taking upon himself the entire kingdom if need be. He was a boy beyond his youth. King Runmari wondered how he obtained such wisdom without the help of his father, King Degnal. It was customary throughout the Great Lands for a king to raise a king, after all.

Prince Oban walked majestically towards King Runmari and simply nodded a gesture of greeting to him. King Runmari nodded back holding back a smile of approval. He admired the way the little Prince conducted himself. Prince Oban never wavered at being pleasant yet forceful and in control.

Then Prince Oban went and sat upon his throne a few feet away from the table of guests. That was his way of conveying that he was not there to socialize per se. It also let everyone know that he was indeed a member of the royal family and not subject to anyone's commands, least of all an outsider.

Prince Oban nodded to Advisor Burton and the advisor nodded to the band who began to play music again.

As the music played, all those in the hall continued to eat and to talk amongst themselves. Although the Prince sat aloft from them, no one ignored his presence.

"He is quite an impressive young Prince," King Runmari whispered to Advisor Burton.

"Yes, King Runmari, yes he is," Advisor Burton agreed, "Well versed in languages, reading, the mathematics, and music. He is an apt student in all subjects," he concluded.

"All subjects?" King Runmari asked mischievously.

"Why yes," replied Advisor Burton.

King Runmari continued eating and merely smiled.

"Do those subjects include weaponry and combat?" King Runmari asked.

At that the music stopped playing in the Autumn Hall and all eyes looked upon Prince Oban once more. He had risen from his throne and was walking directly toward King Runmari. Everyone stood up again and bowed their heads.

Prince Oban stepped in front of King Runmari and without saying a word willed King Runmari to lift his lowered head. Once King Runmari did so, Prince Oban spoke.

"Why does the King wish to know about my studies?" asked the little Prince.

King Runmari smirked at the realization that the Prince could hear a whispered conversation within a hall filled with playing music and chatter.

"My Prince," said King Runmari, "I meant you no disrespect. It is merely an inquiry at your progress in your learning."

After King Runmari answered the Prince's question, he then studied the Prince's reaction to his words. Once again, Prince Oban showed no sign upon his face of what he was thinking. King Runmari was moved, thinking that Prince Oban was even better than he was at hiding his true emotions. As he pondered that notion, to his surprise, Prince Oban suddenly smiled at him. At first, King Runmari was taken aback. For Prince Oban's smile was childlike, youthful and carefree. King Runmari wondered why this sudden change in his behavior. He didn't trust it.

"I train daily with my father's imperial fighting guards, King Runmari," Prince Oban told him.

"Very pleased to hear that you are being readied for your royal duties as King of Degnal Kingdom, Prince Oban..." King Runmari said in the most sincere way he could fashion, "…very pleased."

Prince Oban nodded once, turned on his heels and strolled out of the Autumn Hall without saying another word. His entourage of guards and servants followed closely behind. King Runmari watched as they exited hoping the concern on his face would not show. Nothing happened that might have caused him such anxiety, and yet he didn't feel at ease about his encounter with the Prince nonetheless. He decided that with the continuing of the festivities he'd use that time to probe a little deeper into the mystery that was Prince Oban. He realized that his decision not to attack Degnal Palace and kill everyone in it off was a good one. For then he would have never met such a unique person, that of Prince Oban.

Unfortunately, during the remainder of the evening, King Runmari couldn't get any more information from his hosts about the Prince. In fact, as soon as the Prince exited from the Autumn Hall, dancers arrived, the music became clamorous and the wine was replaced with flaming goblets of beer. It was almost as if the Prince gave his blessing for the entire palace to celebrate with abandon. Before King Runmari knew it, everyone was drunk, including himself and he was being escorted to the visitors' wing of the palace for the night. All of this was new to him. By this time in his visits, he'd already be sleeping in the bed of the conquered King surrounded by the old King's wives and/or mistresses.

CHAPTER 6. Later that night, at a Degnal Kingdom village local inn, King Degnal sat perfectly still after having been awaked sharply out of a sound sleep.

He was abed alone that evening for he was troubled during that day's supper and even declined to drink any wine as he dined. He explained this change from his normal routine by expressing an over indulgence of both the prior night. His men gave him a hearty laugh and a cheer, but unbeknownst to them, the King had felt a chill of late that sunk profoundly within his bones. At first he believed it to be merely the impending winter, predicted to come in bitterly cold and stay far too long. As time wore on though the King knew better than to think that his altered state had anything to do with mere climate changes. Something was gnawing at him and he didn't quite know what. If he allowed himself to explore deeper into his own condition, he would have simply called this new feeling fear; yet, he had never felt weak from fear a day in his life and wondered if perhaps it was an actual sickness that had taken a hold of him.

So, he set out that morning and secretly met with a priestess while it was yet under the cover of night. He had great hope that she'd help him to uncover the truth of his malaise. She didn't disappoint. The priestess gave her royal client a full and thorough examination, upon which, she ruled out the prevailing ailments of the day: pox, fever, malaria, and the like; and even tested for some diseases she had knowledge of from foreign lands. She checked around and about his body, his teeth, hands, his scalp and even the soles of his feet. Then she lit a fire using a mixture of cannabis and myrrh to call forth the ancients. The King and the priestess breathed the aroma in deeply. The ancients would assist them in seeking answers straight from the King's very spirit. As the priestess entered a trance to consult the dead, King Degnal sank into the straw bedding on the floor and finally relaxed. He knew that this ritual would take a while. Everyone knew that the ancients were far wiser than anyone who still walked the earth. He anticipated some sound doctrine from them, something that would immediately take away his ill at ease condition. Unfortunately for him, it wasn't long before the priestess returned to herself and sat upright. Then she mixed another concoction and threw it upon the fire. Afterwards, she brewed a special tea for the King to drink.

"This will calm you, my King," the priestess told him.

The sun had already risen and the villagers were already out and about conducting their daily business. King Degnal grew anxious, but waited patiently for the priestess' findings.

Although the priestess had spent a lengthy time carefully examining the King, the only thing she found was that the King was as healthy as a lion; she told him so directly.

"My King, you are as healthy as a lion," the priestess said proudly.

King Degnal did not know how he felt about the results. He, of course, desired good health, but the diagnosis didn't cure him of his dark mood.

He gently nodded to the priestess as a gesture of thanks, then reached into his battle armor and pulled out a satchel full of silver. As he rose to leave, he tossed the cloth bag onto the straw.

"You're too kind, my King," repeated the priestess over and over again bowing politely as King Degnal exited from her hut. The priestess was then warned repeatedly by the King's guards that if anyone found out about the King's visit, her head would be delivered to the ancients without her body.

King Degnal ventured away from the hut feeling disappointed. He hadn't come any closer to discovering the origin of his uneasiness. However, whatever its source, he wouldn't let any of it show to anyone, especially not to his men. Even if he were upon his death bed, as King he would only display the greatest presentation of strength to the bitter end.

To his dismay, after breakfast, King Degnal found very little peace conducting his daily activities that day. It was more of the same as it had been for many, many moons. The repetition of it all had begun to dull his senses. The weight of all he had done while searching for his only daughter was finally catching up with him. He finally realized that his tactics were not yielding him any results save destruction. He looked out of the chamber window and saw charred land and destroyed homes, homes that he and his men had seized and ruined.

He thought of cancelling his agenda and retiring to

his bed for the remainder of the day. His Commander approached just as he was about to give the order.

"My King, we have sought and found another man claiming to have knowledge of Princess Asha's whereabouts," Commander Testlar informed the King.

King Degnal's hopes of ever finding his daughter alive had long since been dashed. He was now merely searching for what he believed was her body so that he could respectfully bury her in the royal cemetery. He waved a gesture to Commander Testlar giving him permission to bring in the man in question.

Two guards walked a man in before King Degnal and thrust him upon the floor. King Degnal glanced ever so slightly at the man, noting immediately that the man hadn't any eyes.

"Is this a joke?" King Degnal asked angrily.

"My King!" Commander Testlar said snapping to attention, "Why no, my King."

Commander Testlar shot a stern look at his First Lieutenant, "How dare you bring this before our King!" he shouted at him. The First Lieutenant immediately turned to the man and barked "Speak man…" he said shoving him to the floor, "…NOW!"

The man struggled, desperately rolling around trying to right himself into a standing position. Once he was up, he cleared his throat and opened his mouth to speak as he was told but only grunts and groans came out. Everyone looked upon him as if they misunderstood what he was saying. He opened his mouth again as if he was trying earnestly to tell them something. Again, all everyone heard was noise. It quickly became clear to all present that he hadn't a tongue either.

King Degnal recoiled. Then he leaned far forward in order to look the First Lieutenant squarely in the eye before ordering to have his head cut off. But just as the King was about to speak, there came a sudden commotion taking place at the chamber entrance. A rustling sound and muffled shrieks were heard as if from a struggle. Someone was fighting against being restrained. It quickly became clear that whoever this someone was, they were trying to gain entry into the chamber.

"I must gain entry! Let me in!" a girl screamed.

She was being forcefully pushed back, but with her slight frame she somehow managed to break free long enough to run forward.

"That's my father!" she yelled, "Please, my King!"

she screamed, "He can't speak!"

"Let her in," King Degnal demanded.

Moments later, at the King's request, a peasant girl entered the chamber carrying with her a handful of bread. The bread was filthy. It had been tossed to the ground along with her. Each time it fell from her hands, she quickly picked it back up and now brought it in with her wrapped within her dress. She looked a pitiful sight before the King.

Immediately she raced forward, searching the chamber for her father. Finding him standing before the King, she stood at his side. She reached over and took her father's hand and carefully placed some bread in it. He hugged the girl. Then he cried as he sloppily gobbled up the food. The First Lieutenant finally had to pull them apart and forcibly face them toward the King.

The King said nothing as this all transpired. He waited calmly. Something about these events intrigued him.

"Young girl, is this your father?" the King asked.

"Yes…" the girl replied, "…he is, my King."

"Progress," joked the King and everyone briefly laughed.

Then King Degnal nodded to Commander Testlar to

continue with the investigation.

"Girl, we have been informed that your father knows something about the whereabouts of the Princess, Asha. Is this true?" Commander Testlar asked sternly.

The girl looked at her father and reached for his hand. The First Lieutenant moved to stop her, but Commander Testlar gave him a signal to stand down. The girl pressed her hand into that of her father's and began making symbols with her fingers upon it. King Degnal had seen this once before with villagers who would make up secret codes in order to confuse his guards. He couldn't imagine why they thought they were smart enough to out think his men. Everyone knew that his royal army would always have the upper hand. Nonetheless, the King and his men allowed the girl and her father their moment of discussion amongst themselves. Finally, the girl looked up and spoke. Everyone was surprised by her response.

"Yes," she whispered.

The entire chamber rustled in movement including King Degnal. He rose from his chair and stepped forward toward the girl and her father.

"Speak up," he bade her.

"Yes," she replied more emphatically, "He did, he

thinks, encounter Princess Asha."

"Encounter?" King Degnal asked, probing for a better understanding of the girl's answers.

"Tell your King what you know, girl!" Commander Testlar shouted at her.

The girl swallowed hard and began to babble incoherently under her breath.

"Your King is waiting!" Commander Testlar screamed and the girl slowed down her speech.

"…I said…I said…that my father loves the forest…" she gulped, "…especially at night when the moon is out…" she paused while nervously looking around.

Everyone was listening to her and hanging upon her every word, "…So much so…" she paused, "…So much so…that he goes out alone most nights to walk about. I try to tell him not to but he doesn't listen…" she paused again, "…One night while out walking, he grew tired and decided to rest on a rock…" she said, "…that's when he overheard two men talking about the Princess, Princess Asha. And as he listened to them talk, that's when he became very afraid."

"Girl…" King Degnal drew nearer to her and asked, "…why was your father afraid? Answer me!" he barked harshly then quickly corrected himself by waving an apology.

In stark fear of the King, the girl pressed on.

"He became afraid, my King…" she bowed, "…because…because he began to think that she, the Princess, might actually be with them, the men, and that it wasn't just talk," the girl told the King.

The entire chamber gasped at the hearing of the girl's words. The very thought of it was the best and the worst news they had heard throughout their entire search for the King's daughter. Yet, would they dare themselves to believe anything the girl said? King Degnal considered carefully what next to ask.

"Why did your father believe that it wasn't just…just…talk?" asked the King.

He was gentler in his manner this time while confronting her. Truth was, she was beginning to spark something in him that he hadn't felt in quite some time – hope. He didn't believe that this day would ever come. He was finally getting close to having an answer about his daughter.

"Because, my King, one of the men asked her if she was hungry?" the girl answered.

The King stared at the peasant girl for a lengthy

amount of time before inquiring any further. He couldn't help but think about the enormous time spent torturing his villagers, the arrests, the killings. To think that, all the while, this simple child had just given them their only credible lead. King Degnal took another moment to formulate his thoughts.

"Did my Asha answer these men?" King Degnal asked with a small crack in his voice.

The girl began to nod before opening her mouth to answer, "Yes, my King," she replied, "Princess Asha said 'yes.'" The girl's father shook his head in agreement once his daughter finished telling the story. He hesitated, out of respect for his King, to reach out to hug his daughter. King Degnal motioned to the First Lieutenant that they could do so. The girl grabbed her father and they embraced.

"Leave me," King Degnal demanded in a whisper.

Then he slowly walked back to his seat, sat down and rested his head in his hand. Commander Testlar gave orders to his First Lieutenant to escort the father and his daughter out of the chamber.

Moments later, the entire room was empty, save for the King. He alone sat in perfect contemplation and quiet.

The recent events, unfortunately, only added another degree of weariness to his already burdened soul. Gone were the days of running out after every clue. He wanted to mull news over for a while these days. He might even allow himself to sleep on it. Then, when refreshed, he'd plan his next move with a well thought out strategy.

Commander Testlar was just outside the door giving orders that the King was not to be disturbed without consulting the Commander first. Then, with the corridors clear, Commander Testlar walked in and approached the King.

"My King," Commander Testlar said, alerting the King of his presence.

King Degnal lifted his head and stared past his Commander.

"Can we trust it?" King Degnal asked.

"My King, I've already instructed guards to accompany the father into the forest. They will trace his steps and search the entire area," Commander Testlar informed the King.

King Degnal nodded his approval, then turned back around and continued to think heavily about the possibility of finally finding his daughter.

"Yes, but can you trust this tale?" the King asked again.

"I believe so, my King…" Commander Testlar said, "…I believe that it is trustworthy this time."

King Degnal took his supper alone that evening and ate very little of it. He nearly collapsed upon the bed halfway through the meal and fell into a terrible slumber. His sleep was restless, his mind raced. He was overwhelmed with thoughts of what might have happened to his daughter. She was just a little girl at the time of her abduction. Now, she would be at the age to wed. He had looked forward to arranging hers and fortifying alliances. It angered him unrelentingly to suppose that someone had taken that simple pleasure away from him. He was the King! He was her father.

With thoughts of his daughter swimming through his mind, there came something unusual that began to creep in underneath. It was an echo of sorts seemingly coming from his own subconscious mind, but not something that he had ever heard before. At first, it was like a thick but tiny shadow, the size of a prick. It grew wider in perceptibility. Then it spread rapidly across his brain. As it grew in mass, it blanketed the King with warmth he hadn't felt since he was a young boy. He enjoyed it. He began to sleep more soundly. Then…

"Come home," said a voice in the King's mind.

The King felt as if the voice was coming out from his very own heart. The small voice bellowed softly as a whisper, then loudly as a cry, echoing over and over again.

"Come home…" it said, "…Come home! COME HOME!"

All the while, the King slept in a cozy, but eerie haze.

"We are under attack!" said the voice, but this time audibly.

King Degnal shot straight up and looked about his dark chamber. Then he jumped out of bed and began searching everywhere. He knew in his mind that no one was in there with him, but he could have sworn that he heard someone's voice. He turned over furniture and looked behind the drapes. Then he flung open the door. His two guards snapped to attention.

"My King!" they said in unison.

King Degnal nodded to them and then retreated back

inside. As he walked over to his bed again and sat upon it, he began to think that he must have been dreaming. He also gathered that it was unlike any dream he had ever had in all his days. To him, it was as if someone was leaning over him as he slept and speaking directly into his ear.

King Degnal was so shaken by the voice in his head, that before dawn, he and three-quarters of his guards rallied together and rode straight out of the village toward home, Degnal Palace.

"My King, men are still combing the forest and will continue as requested," Commander Testlar told the King, riding alongside him through the fields.

"Thank you, Commander Testlar," King Degnal said.

"My King, why the sudden change in plans?" Commander Testlar asked.

King Degnal did not hesitate in answering his top guard.

"We're under attack!" he replied.

Commander Testlar saluted the King, then without question, turned sharply and sent word through the ranks to ride and ride hard. The language he used conveyed an immediate understanding that they would not stop during their journey until they reached the gates of the palace.

CHAPTER 7. Kenneth has but one season – winter; brisk, frosty, frigid winters. Visitors and would be marauders consider its climate unbearable. Kenneth has been protected for centuries for this reason. They were fortunate to never have to use their army for military purposes.

Kenneth's vast territory stretches out from ocean to ocean at the northern most peak of the Great Lands. Nearly all of its surface area is dominated by glaciers, the rest by jagged boulders and densely populated snow-capped mountainous topography. Its several lakes are at most times frozen over solid. Its trees are bare with ice capsules hanging from their branches. Even crops don't grow in its rocky soil without continual care through fertilization. Vegetables are cultivated in hot huts in order to shield seeds from freezing temperatures. From a distance, the landscape appears uninhabitable. Yet, it is home to polar bears, moose, reindeer, walruses, and humans.

Its population is a mere ninety thousand persons

including women and children, much smaller than other kingdoms. Residents there manage to live through the blistery cold from sun to sun, with a few new moons of autumns to break up the monotony. These autumns, blessed breaks from the constant chill, are considered summers to the Kenneth people. During such times, they go swimming in the temporarily thawed streams and lakes, and roast deer on spits in celebration of this warmth with their neighbors.

Another advantage of living in Kenneth and braving its exceedingly frosty elements is that it made its people exceptionally strong. Their bodies are powerfully muscular regardless of age, their skin, tough and rugged. Additionally, they are also extraordinarily tall. Some believe the Kenneth people developed this way over time out of sheer necessity. Enduring the harsh weather has developed and equipped them physically to do so.

Kenneth's form of government is unique as well. They do not have a king. Instead they have a small group of village elders who make all important decisions on behalf of the people. The Council of Elders, as it is called, convene on the eve of every new moon to discuss any issues relevant to Kenneth. The item on the agenda this day was about the brutal attack of two of their own. Two men were in the act of trading supplies in the south, when, for no legitimate reason, they were viciously assaulted.

Elders Isoba and Duna were engaged in a heated debate with Elders Nafari, and Sam. These two sets of elders were at odds against each other over what they should do in retaliation of this egregious insult to their kinsmen. Two wanted revenge, while the others wanted to maintain peaceful alliances with their neighbors. The other twelve elders could have been persuaded either way.

"We've been at peace long enough!" Elder Isoba shouted, "I say, this time we fight!"

"I agree!" Elder Duna concurred angrily.

Elders Nafari and Sam disagreed strongly, and grimaced at Elder Isoba's harsh words. They had already expressed their opinions vehemently to the rest when the day began. It was sunset and the talks seemed without compromise.

"How many ways can I say that a war would leave us vulnerable here at home," Elder Nafari pleaded, "We just can't risk it."

"An attack on our own land would destroy us all!" Elder Sam chimed in.

The other twelve elders shook their heads in

agreement. Though everyone knew that the likelihood of any kingdom wishing to evade them was highly unlikely, they didn't want to take that chance.

"Are we cowards?" shouted Elder Isoba.

Elder Isoba lived through nineteen horrific, catastrophic storms; storms so bad, they nearly annihilated the entire Kenneth territory. Isoba survived them all by nestling his entire family into a cave at the side of a mountain that he dug with his bare hands. When the storm had ended, it took him three whole sun cycles to dig the family back out due to an avalanche of snow. Everyone in his clan lived to tell the tale. He was the proud father of fourteen sons and five daughters, twenty-three grandchildren and eleven great grandchildren. He was the most senior of all the elders and although there wasn't a real hierarchy within the elder council, he was the one that everyone heeded the most.

In truth, Elder Isoba wasn't intentionally trying to sway the others to his way of thinking. He was just angry, having been one of the first people to see the two merchants return to Kenneth after their attack. He couldn't believe his eyes.

"You saw them. You saw the condition they were

in..." he said, sighing with regret at what he had witnessed, "...They had their eyes gouged out."

"And their tongues!" Elder Duna shouted.

The other elders scowled at the horror of it all. The two merchants barely made it back home alive. They traveled most of their journey on foot, because on top of losing critical parts of their bodies, they also were robbed of their property and their horses. When they arrived, the ancient Kenneth priest, Godlumthakathi, was summoned to care for them.

Godlumthakathi went to work immediately treating their wounds with a mixture of honey and cannabis resin. He then applied healing balms of aloe to soothe their skin. Of course, he couldn't restore their missing eyes or their tongues, but he did manage to ease some of their suffering by taking them to the hot springs for warm, relaxing baths. This worked well as a sedative, as the priest knew they needed many, many new moons of rest.

Directly after Godlumthakathi ministered to the mutilated men, the Elders thoroughly investigated their tale of woe. Though, it was nearly impossible to extract much information from them without the use of sight, or speech. Unfortunately, neither merchant was adept at writing. They were laborers, simple, common folk. They had never learned to read or write formally, having never been to school. Each only knew enough to recognize territory markers and village signs. Anything further than that was out of their capabilities. Nonetheless, the Elders were successful at finding out what happened to them.

It was Elder Sam's idea to shout out the names of kingdoms in the Great Lands, telling the men to nod "yes" when he mentioned the one that destroyed their lives. When he got to Degnal Kingdom, both men vehemently shook their heads affirming the place where everything went wrong for them.

"…They couldn't even tell us who did this to them!" he paused, "…We need to strike back and we need to strike back hard!" Elder Duna continued.

"We cannot win a war against the Degnal Kingdom…" Elder Nafari said to the council, "…We do not have tens of thousands of men in our army, as you all know."

"Nafari is right. They are hundreds of thousands of men strong. How can we possibly compete with such a great number?" asked Elder Sam.

At that, all of the elders lowered their heads in

contemplation. They knew with regret that a day such as this would come. This incident marked a defining moment. Do they show that they can defend their kind or do they become the weakest sovereignty in the Great Lands? They had no skill at war. They had never even sent their army out to do battle.

"It is true, kinsmen, we are at a disadvantage…" said Elder Isoba gravely, "…but let us not concentrate on lack, however difficult that may be…"

The elders lifted their heads while listening to Elder Isoba.

"…We may be out-numbered, but one of our kinds can beat ten of theirs. We all know this to be true. Besides, our sheer size alone will drive most of them away in terror…Plus, although not tried, we are as well trained for battle as they…" he continued.

They all knew what was said about them, that many feared their size and strength, and the Kennethians had always used this perception to their full advantage. They also knew that their weaponry was unlike any others, using metals and poisons at the tips of their spears was revolutionary. However, with this latest theft of their merchants, the elders realized that Degnal Kingdom now possessed these secrets too. No one doubted that Degnal had already begun production of similar arms. With that realization, the council started becoming swayed by Elder Isoba's words.

"…And, let us not forget our greatest weapon…" Elder Isoba said to his now captive audience.

The elders knew exactly of what he was referring to – magic.

"…It's one that no one knows about throughout these Great Lands," Elder Isoba said with a grin.

The Elders shook at the thought of such a drastic measure. Side conversations sprung up throughout the hut. The Kenneth law was put in place against such practices for their own protection. It was forbidden for them to summon these other worldly forces; the consequences were far too extreme. For every request made to Priest Godlumthakathi to act on their behalf for these dark dealings, the price had to be paid for with someone's flesh. In other words, someone would have to die in order for their wish to be fulfilled. The Elders took these matters seriously and longed for none to perish in this manner.

"…I know…it's not my desire to see anyone suffer either for the sake of the whole, but we can't allow other kingdoms to think they can just do these things to us and get away with them," Elder Isoba told them.

"We all know that Elder Isoba does not suggest war easily ..." Elder Duna nodded politely to Elder Isoba, "...And neither do I, but look at the alternative...If we do nothing, we would truly be vulnerable to invaders. Just because these kingdoms find our territory hard to bear doesn't mean they don't want to possess it. They will not think twice of taking our people and using them as slaves either."

"The thought is unimaginable, but Elder Duna is right..." Elder Isoba said, "...Many could be carted off and forced into hard labor. May the gods help us if that day ever comes."

Until this point, Elders Nafari and Sam had vehemently argued against the possibility of war, but they were now warming up to the idea.

"Of course, gentlemen, trading with Degnal would cease," Elder Isoba warned.

The hut erupted again with side conversations. Elder Isoba had clearly struck a nerve with the council. They enjoyed the things they received through trade; things like herbs, spices, breads, and especially wine - one of their favorite imports. The thought of not being able to conduct trade gave them all pause.

To their dismay, Kenneth had very few luxuries. They were outdoorsmen at heart and enjoyed it all immensely. However, given the nature of living at the top of the world, their lives were shaped by the words, 'weather permitting.' At those times they stayed indoors under thatched roofs, huddled beneath heavily blanketed animal furs. Were it not for the items that came in from neighboring territories, life could be exceedingly boring in Kenneth.

"I concede..." Elder Nafari blurted reluctantly, "...we do need to go to war with...Degnal."

Elder Sam nodded in agreement. He knew that Kenneth would cease to be a kingdom if they were looked upon as weaklings.

"We are not weaklings," Elder Sam uttered quietly.

"No...no, we are not," Elder Isoba agreed.

"Aye!" shouted all the other elders in unison.

"We will speak to Priest Godlumthakathi at sunrise..." said Elder Isoba, "...I look forward to what he has in store for our enemies."

The Kenneth Elder Council went on to discuss what they would say to their people and how they would go about preparing their army. Without a king, it was up to them to think about such things regarding the territory. The army would begin training immediately. They didn't want to waste any time now that they were all on one accord. They would gather supplies from their people in order to send their men off fully equipped for the battle ahead.

No one mentioned the consequence of using magic. Aside from all of the things that needed to be done in preparation for war, the elders also had to decide who among them would have to give their life. They needed to ensure victory for the spell Priest Godlumthakathi would cast.

CHAPTER 8. King Runmari awoke leisurely in the visitors' wing of the palace, feeling quite satisfied with himself and with his substantially marvelous findings of the Degnal Kingdom. 'This will all soon be mine,' he thought, taking great pleasure in the idea of seizing this kingdom indeed. Fortunately for him, he really didn't have to do much at all to take it. He hadn't done anything so far and yet the circumstances were lining up perfectly in his favor. In his mind, it was practically being handed to him as a gift, with their king and army still a long way off, having no interest of returning back home any time soon. He thought, 'The Degnal people will welcome a new king at this point.' He surmised that they might even request he stay and assume the kingship. 'Wouldn't that be marvelous?' he grinned.

Yes, Degnal Kingdom would be one of the easiest lands King Runmari ever acquired. He wouldn't even have to enact his usual display of killings and terrorizing. To ensure his success in this area, he devised a plot to manipulate the situation even further to his advantage. He decided that he'd prey on their fears. He'd begin by making subtle suggestions to the Degnal Advisors during their morning meal. He'd relay to them a story of utter chaos throughout the Great Lands. He would make it sound as if their kingdom might be too exposed to threats. He'd tell tall tales of intruders roving around and menacing territories, stories of ransacking and pillaging. He'd paint an ugly picture of woe. The gods knew he had enough material of his own escapades to draw from. He would scare them to death and make their hearts flutter with dread.

He rolled over on the plush bed he had just slept in and practically roared with laughter to himself. As he did so, Degnal servants drew him a bath, lifted him up and escorted him gently into a tub of piping hot water. King Runmari considered this an indulgence, however pleasurable. Though, once submerged, he was washed by three beautiful ladies who scrubbed him from head to toe in a rhythmic pattern that both cleansed and massaged. Despite himself, King Runmari enjoyed it thoroughly and did not wish it to end.

As the water grew colder, the ladies coasted him out of the vessel and dried him off by patting his body down with rose petals. Then a male servant dressed him in clean silks, the likes of which King Runmari wouldn't be caught dead wearing in his lands. He was the supreme chief of his army, a warrior. He preferred a suit of armor to the likes of these garments that cooled in unmentionable areas and warmed him in others. Still he conceded to the Degnal Kingdom's sensibilities in order to experience the full essence of their ways.

So far, he had been wined and dined and entertained in a manner that, although not completely foreign to him, wasn't exactly everyday fare in his own realm. In truth, King Runmari found most of it to be extravagant and wasteful, preferring instead the field of battle. Degnal Kingdom seemed to him the land of self-indulgence. To him, even the Degnal servants appeared to have an air of it. Most never bothered lowering their heads in his presence, an attitude he noted with disgust. They were respectful, of course, but they did not conduct themselves in the humility of which he was accustomed. He vowed to himself that once he took Degnal Kingdom, he would break their spirits immediately and make sure that they knew him as their king and sovereign lord. He would not be satisfied until his new subjects feared him with every fiber of their beings, and until he saw nothing but panic stricken faces when he was in their presence.

Once King Runmari was fully dressed, he was escorted through the corridors of the Degnal Palace. He looked upon every inch of it with a sense of pride, for in his mind, it was about to be his. The marble floors, the hand sculpted, divinely inspired, carved plaster pillars, constructed by talented artisans, and finely painted portraits of the Degnal legacy, all exquisitely executed. 'Those portraits will be replaced,' he thought. The palace possessed all manner of opulence and attention to detail at every turn. King Runmari felt warmly gleeful at the thought of possessing it all.

Around another section of the palace, he saw large windows stretching across an area twenty arms' length long. At a distance was Degnal's abundantly picturesque landscape. It was a spectacular sight for the senses. He couldn't help but appreciate the majesty and grandeur of it all. Below was a reflection of it in some of the more than twelve pools surrounding the Palace.

As he walked further, the Degnal Palace garden came into view, equipped with well sculptured monuments of plaster celebrating the Degnal Empire in grand style.

King Runmari looked down and marveled at its lushness and beauty. Though he was not a man who necessarily took any care to something as delicate as a flower, how could he not love the way these were presented? It was a work of art - a maze of hedges interspersed with blooming palms, ubiquitous jacaranda, and avocado trees. In the heart of each section were bountiful bushes of roses, lilac, orchid, fern, five-hundred varieties of camellia, and other brightly colored floras. To King Runmari, it looked like an oasis for the gods planted on earth. He decided right then and there that he would make this palace his new home in his expanded kingdom, or at the very least, his summer retreat after battles.

Degnal Palace was enormous too. King Runmari entered yet another part of it at its west side. According to the Degnal guards, they were heading towards the Summer Hall. King Runmari grinned at the thought of it. He took the hall's name as yet another sign of his good fortune – literally. Had he not just thought of that very same season?

As they rounded this other corridor, a dramatic sight came upon them, the Degnal Kingdom's mountains, called Atlas, after the god of bounty. Their breadth was awe-inspiring. King Runmari had acquired kingdoms with mountains before but none as grandiose as these. These were so tall that clouds swallowed their peaks. King Runmari stopped for a moment to take it all in. He hadn't seen them clearly from the road. It was late approaching sunset, when he entered the Degnal Palace, and he was admittedly weary from his journey. Seeing them at dusk did not give them justice.

In the light of day, however, the sheer range of them could not be measured. King Runmari tried to determine how wide they extended to his left and to his right and was unable to do so. He inhaled deeply and tried to squelch a roaring laugh. He knew he'd be undefeatable with mountains such as these, for there wasn't an army in all of the Great Lands who would attempt to cross them. King Runmari pulled himself away from the window quickly. He didn't want anyone to see the broad smile spreading menacingly across his face.

Then King Runmari, the Degnal guards and a few of his own approached the Summer Hall. At less than five steps away, the doors opened seamlessly upon their arrival. The Degnal servants weren't to King Runmari's liking, but he did find them extremely efficient.

He entered the hall and was immediately greeted by Advisor Burton, whom King Runmari now knew as the head advisor.

"I hope you slept well, King Runmari?" Advisor Burton asked.

"Yes, thank you," said King Runmari cordially, "Very."

"Please, take a seat here at the head of our humble table," Advisor Burton told King Runmari, while fanning his arm out at a table half the size of the chamber and to a chair that was fit for a king.

Advisor Burton was giving him the very seat of their King! King Runmari grinned to himself, thinking that this might be the easiest conquest in his illustrious career.

King Runmari sat down proudly upon the impressive chair. It was made of pure silver with precious gemstones studded down its sides, and cushioned in deep blue and purple velvet fabric. King Runmari thought humorously, 'Now all I need is King Degnal's crown.'

The Degnal Advisors and the noblemen present took their seats as well. They greeted King Runmari as if he were an old friend and engaged him in conversation that was both light, cheerful and warm-hearted.

Advisor Burton lowered his head and musicians began to play for the diners. Then everyone present concentrated on the meal. The enormous table was laden with, what could only be described as a feast. King Runmari thought, 'I could get used to this.' Between the food, drink and melodies, King Runmari found himself being lulled into an almost dream-like state. At times, to his chagrin, he even felt as if he was a part of the Degnal people and their ever festive customs.

Suddenly, the doors of the Summer Hall opened and the Degnal Royal Announcer stepped inside.

"All honor to the King, King Degnal!" the announcer shouted.

Everyone quickly jumped to their feet, everyone that is, except King Runmari. As a king himself, he never had to rise before another. Yet, that wasn't the reasoning of him remaining in his seat.

To King Runmari's surprise, Degnal's long gone King entered the Summer Hall in all his glory, followed by his entourage of Commander Testlar and no less than one-hundred members of his royal guards. King Runmari slowly lifted himself from the beautifully decorated chair. As he did so, he saw King Degnal staring directly at him from across the room.

King Runmari couldn't help the stunned look he had on his face, though he tried not to let it show. All he could think about was how fast King Degnal and his riders must have rode in order to make it back to the palace so quickly. Last he heard from his spies, King Degnal was at least a seven days ride away. He wondered if it was just a coincidence that he had returned suddenly or if someone somehow discovered his secret plan and sent word. He wanted to look the Degnal Advisors squarely in the eye in order to detect which one might have done so, but their heads were still bowed. At that, he got hold of himself and walked toward King Degnal.

"Greetings, King Degnal," King Runmari said with a hand flourish.

"King Runmari…" King Degnal said nodding his head as a gesture of greeting, "…I hope your visit here has been a good one."

King Degnal then strolled around the table greeting his Advisors. Each Advisor said a few warm words to their king. Everyone was happy to see him back home. His royal nobles cheered as their King circled around the crowd.

"My King, it is so good to see you," said one Advisor.

"My King, you do look well," said another.

"My King, it's been too long without you," Advisor Burton told him.

"Yes, my old friend…" King Degnal agreed, "…it has. Are things well here at home?"

King Degnal asked this question while walking toward the head of the table.

"My King, we have had the blessings of your good leadership and protection extended to us in your absence…" Advisor Burton told him, "…We are indebted to you for our continued peace…"

King Runmari turned around to go back to his seat. He was shocked to see that his plate and drink had been removed. A fresh setting sat in its place.

"…The rest we may discuss in chamber, my King," Advisor Burton concluded.

"Yes, we shall," King Degnal agreed as he took his seat at the head of the table, the very same chair previously occupied by King Runmari.

When King Degnal sat, others followed suit and took their seats as well. Meanwhile, one of the King's Advisors ushered King Runmari to the end of the long table, quite a distance away from the King. Although King Runmari was seething with anger, he graciously followed the Advisor. He couldn't help but note that he would now be seated with some of the lesser nobles of the Degnal realm. He was a smart man and knew that this was an intentional slight. In this new position at the table, he would have to shout to be heard by the King. Again, he wondered how King Degnal knew about his very secret intentions. He hadn't mentioned anything to anyone, not even to his spies. He began to think that they might have put together the scenario themselves of his desire to have Degnal Kingdom, though he believed them incapable of coming up with that conclusion on their own. At any rate, he would get to the bottom of this betrayal and the culprit or culprits would be punished severely, of that King Runmari was sure.

Firstly though, he had to make a smooth exit. He knew that he had to do so without bringing attention to the real reason he had ventured to Degnal Kingdom. With that in mind, he straightened up and began paying closer attention to everything and everyone before him. It never eluded him that there were at least one-hundred Degnal armed guards in the Summer Hall and that his small brigade was probably surrounded outside.

"King Runmari…" King Degnal began, and everyone in the hall grew silent, "…what brings you to our modest territory?"

King Runmari thought, 'Modest? Hardly,' he mused, then, 'Ah, here it comes,' thinking King Degnal might not allow him to leave Degnal Kingdom with his life.

"Oh gracious, King Degnal, you are so kind…" King Runmari said, mustering as much good will as he could, "…I am a traveler, as you know…"

The truth was, King Runmari wasn't sure what King Degnal knew about him, but he aired on the side of caution. He would not pretend to be anything other than what he now believed King Degnal knew – that he was notorious for acquiring kingdoms in the Great Lands.

"…I have only come this great distance to see for myself what others have told me about," King Runmari said truthfully.

The others present were now completely engrossed in the Kings' conversation. The Degnal people astutely heard in their King a particular tone that signified wariness of King Runmari's motives.

"And what have you been told, King Runmari? Surely, nothing so great as to have you travel so far away from your other…kingdoms?" King Degnal asked, emphasizing the word 'kingdoms.'

King Runmari grinned, adsorbing the full weight of King Degnal's subtle intention. 'He wishes to catch me in a lie,' King Runmari thought. He would ease his way out of this situation the same way he had on many other occasions. Though a warrior, King Runmari was a consummate negotiator, skilled in diplomacy. Though brutal in his ways, he was by all accounts also a king in his own right. He knew what to say in any given circumstance.

"I have heard, same as everyone in the Great Lands that King Degnal is fond of silver and that he possesses more of it than any of the other kingdoms combined," King Runmari replied.

"So, you'd like to see my treasures?" King Degnal said with a laugh.

"As one King to another King, I would never advise you to show yours," King Runmari said also with a laugh.

At that, the entire assembly laughed as well, breaking the tension that they all were experiencing.

"No, no, no…I come bearing gifts, and…" King Runmari said.

"And?" King Degnal asked.

"…and I would like to speak with you about a possible alliance," King Runmari told him, while wondering to himself if King Degnal believed anything he was saying.

"Possible alliance?" King Degnal repeated, pausing briefly and lowering his head.

When he lifted his head again, he had a smile upon his face.

"Advisors, what do we say about alliances?" King Degnal asked, specifically looking over at Advisor Burton.

"We say, my King, alliances need only be forged in battle," Advisor Burton answered King Degnal without looking over at King Runmari.

King Runmari smiled politely, wanting to swiftly exit the hall and return again with his entire army in tow. He kept that thought to himself however, and simply smiled.

"You are a wise king, King Degnal," King Runmari said as agreeably as he could.

King Runmari now knew with confidence that King Degnal was on to him and his schemes. If he made it out of there with his life, he would find the guilty party for this treason and he would make them pay with not only their lives, but with the lives of their entire families as well.

CHAPTER 9. Later that day, King Degnal sat upon his throne, head in hand, boiling over with anger.

"He's gone, my King," Commander Testlar informed him.

King Degnal had been sitting mute since King Runmari's swift departure. By all accounts, no one could figure out why. Though the two Kings' behavior toward one another during the meal had been cool yet cordial, everyone expected such at a first meeting between members of royal families. Everyone knew that King Degnal was use to entertaining, but they surmised that he mightn't have wished to welcome visitors upon so soon returning home. This new found silence challenged everyone around him except Commander Testlar. Testlar had remained in the hall, seated in his usual chair, at the right hand of the King, a few arms length from the throne. The hall had already been forcefully emptied out. He and Advisor Burton were the only ones still present before the King.

"We have placed the gifts he brought in the royal

treasury, as you requested," Advisor Burton said, bowing to his King, and then nodding to Commander Testlar.

He then exited from the chamber as swiftly and quietly as he possibly could. He did not await a response. With so many years in service to the King, he knew when his assistance was no longer required.

Now, only Commander Testlar and King Degnal remained. Commander Testlar was pleased. He had been waiting practically all day since their return to the palace to have a private audience with the King. They would no longer be interrupted.

"How did you know, my wise King?" Commander Testlar asked the instant Advisor Burton abruptly exited.

He was so impressed with his chief, his King, his sovereign Lord. Clearly, there was something new going on with Degnal Kingdom and with his King that had now changed everything.

"...It's as if you somehow knew that King Runmari was here and, not only that he was here, but that he was up to something malevolent!" Commander Testlar said in absolute awe.

King Degnal lifted his head and smiled.

"Have you other spies that I am not aware of?"

Commander Testlar asked humbly.

"If I told you my secret, you would not believe me…" King Degnal told Testlar honestly.

Then he paused. In truth, he too was trying to piece together his own sudden good fortune.

"…It is as magical as the Heavens themselves, I assure you," King Degnal said feeling pretty awed by it all as well.

Commander Testlar always took his King's words literally, so he pondered the King's statement for a few moments, eyeing him to discern the nature of it. He couldn't help feeling perplexed. Meanwhile, King Degnal's face showed no signs of illumination as to the cause of his miraculous foretelling of their Kingdom's impending danger.

"What do we know about King Runmari?" King Degnal asked Testlar.

"There are only rumors about him, none good I'm afraid, my King," Commander Testlar replied.

King Degnal sighed.

"First my only daughter and now this…" he mumbled.

"It is said that he roams freely from kingdom to kingdom taking whatever he wants. He has acquired quite a few lands this way," Commander Testlar said solemnly.

"Acquired or stolen?" King Degnal asked and answered with a wave of his hand.

"My King, he has a great army, powerfully strong and loyal to the death. The stories told of his brutality are known by many unfortunate victims," Commander Testlar told him.

"Why come here with a pretense then? Surely, in my absence he could have done any number of horrific deeds and I would have returned completely unaware?" King Degnal said, almost as if he were just thinking out loud, "It wouldn't have taken much to subdue the scattered forces we had left here, would it?"

"No, my King, indeed," Commander Testlar agreed.

King Degnal and Commander Testlar took a moment and thought about the peril that could have befallen their land in their absence.

"We were on a noble quest, my King..." Commander Testlar said, "...Your daughter will be found and brought back home safely. We will not stop until that has been satisfied and you are made whole again."

Commander Testlar knelt down at King Degnal's feet and allowed a single tear to fall from his eyes. King Degnal placed his hand on Commander Testlar's shoulder and patted it gently. They had been through many battles together, fighting hard and strong, side by side. They were good at it, relentless and self assured, regardless of the obstacles. These new challenges, however, left them tired and weary.

"Yes, Testlar. Yes. We will not lose hope in that task. We must find her. Someone somewhere must know what happened to her. People don't just vanish," King Degnal agreed.

Commander Testlar rose and collected himself. He stood erect again before his King.

"Again I tell you, you were so wise, my King..." Commander Testlar said, "... to have ordered us to return as you had."

Commander Testlar was still awestruck and if he could admit it to himself, he was also a little concerned. It was always his job to inform the King of the goings on around them, not the other way around. He was the one who brought confidences to his King. He was the one who took care of threats that came against the Kingdom. He didn't let it show, but he was beginning to feel slightly inadequate in that area of late. He really needed an answer a bit more substantial than the explanation of the Heavens.

Suddenly, the doors of the Summer Hall burst open and in walked Prince Oban. He was accompanied by a small entourage of servants, tutors, and guards. King Degnal's heart actually skipped a beat at the sight of him. When last he saw the Prince, his son, he was just a baby. He couldn't believe how much he had grown. King Degnal had only seen him that one time during the Naming Ceremony. That very next day, Princess Asha had been stolen away and King Degnal hadn't been home since.

King Degnal felt overwhelmed by how much he had missed in those many winters of his son's growth and development. To him, it was as if Prince Oban had matured overnight. He looked upon him, admiring every aspect. He possessed King Degnal's height, but his face was definitely that of his wife, the Queen Mother. His features were striking, skin as golden as the summer sun. He stood with such poise and confidence, that King Degnal marveled at his every breath. To his delight, his son looked every part a king, dressed in a thick, beautifully tapered robe that covered stylish garments beneath that were tailored to perfection. King Degnal immediately leapt from his chair and marched towards his son.

"My son!" he exclaimed with a tear in his eye.

"My King father, good afternoon," Prince Oban said, equally tearful albeit formal.

King Degnal knelt down on one knee and stretched out his arms. His son, Prince Oban, stepped forward and they embraced each other warmly, each weeping openly. Though Prince Oban hadn't been in the company of his father since birth, he had thoroughly read all about his exploits and his kingship in the palace archives, enjoying each and every volume immensely. It was the stuff of legends. For him, his father, the King, was the most courageous and adventurous warrior king of all time. Though his tutors were commanded to teach him of all the others, to Prince Oban, there was none braver than his father. King Degnal was Prince Oban's hero and seeing him now in the flesh brought all of his fantasies to life. Prince Oban was completely mesmerized. Even when King Degnal released his son, Prince Oban continued to stare at him in wonder.

"My, how you have grown," King Degnal

commented, while escorting Prince Oban to his seat, the one beside the throne.

Prince Oban stepped up and sat in his now favorite chair, the one next to his father. King Degnal looked upon him and smiled proudly, noting that his son truly possessed the intangible air of royalty, the essence of statehood that could not be taught. One had to inherit this quality. Prince Oban reeked of it.

"How have your days been in my absence?" King Degnal asked his son.

"They have been good, my King father…" Prince Oban told him, "…but I have missed you."

"I have missed you as well…" King Degnal said, "…My mission went on longer than…longer than I…than we expected."

"I know that you have looked everywhere throughout the realm, my King father," Prince Oban said in a way that somehow comforted his father.

King Degnal admired the maturity of his son. At times he could have sworn he was conversing with someone his own age.

"I have…" King Degnal said, "…You need not worry about your sister. Though you didn't really know her, you will come to know her in this life time. I assure you of that. She is one of your strongest advocates."

Prince Oban lowered his eyes and scrunched up his lips in a frown. His face donned a doubtful expression.

"Don't you believe your father, the King?" King Degnal asked humorously.

Then the King looked around the chamber and exchanged a chuckle with those present. They laughed with the King about his son's precocious nature. Prince Oban did not answer his father's question. Instead he smiled very politely and nodded until his father changed the subject.

"I see..." King Degnal finally said, acknowledging his son's non verbal desire to shift their topic, "...and your mother, the Queen? How goes it with her?"

"Queen mother comes to visit me every day..." Prince Oban said with a smile, "...She and I love to walk around the gardens, my King father."

"Very good..." King Degnal responded happily, "...They were constructed as a wedding gift to her. I'm pleased she still enjoys them."

At that moment King Degnal realized that he had not seen his wife since his return to the palace. It was unusual for him not to have sent for her, but he had many other pressing matters to attend. He would make it his priority to visit with her in the morning before he started his day. As he thought of these things, Prince Oban stared at him curiously.

"We will start our lessons together very soon, my son. Would you like that?" King Degnal asked.

"I would!" Prince Oban exclaimed excitedly.

"What would you like to begin with first, my son?" King Degnal asked.

"My King father, there are a great many battles that you have won where you were out-numbered, and weary from the fighting, without sleep, food and sometimes without proper cover and still you managed..." Prince Oban blurted rapidly.

"Yes?" King Degnal asked with a smile, awaiting an actual question from his son.

"...Well, I'd like to know how you out-smarted the enemy each and every time..." Prince Oban said, "...Can you tell me how you did that...tonight? That's what I'd like to know first!"

"Tonight?" King Degnal choked in laughter.

"Yes. Please," Prince Oban answered then sat up tall waiting to hear all about his father's exploits.

King Degnal wanted to laugh some more, but glanced over and saw the seriousness upon his son's face. He felt honored that his son was so eager to hear all about him. It made him feel proud that he would have an heir to his throne who would be truly knowledgeable about the richness of the Degnal heritage.

"My son…" King Degnal paused, "…My son, you are a unique child I see…" he told him, "…May we start your lesson with the King on the new moon, after your father has had his rest from travel?" the King asked in his most diplomatic tone.

Prince Oban lowered his head feeling very saddened. He was thinking contemplatively about his father's request. He felt as if he had waited his entire life for an audience with his father, the King. He didn't think he could wait any longer. Yet, despite his anxiousness, he knew that his father was right. He had just returned from a long, grueling journey.

Prince Oban lifted his head to see his father staring back at him. He noticed the gentleness of his father's eyes, the warmth of his smile. He could tell that his father loved him dearly. Prince Oban leapt from his chair and threw his arms around his father's neck and hugged him.

"Of course, my father King…" Prince Oban said practically weeping again, "…Of course. We can start whenever you would like."

"Thank you, my son…" King Degnal told him, "…I am looking forward to our time together. I truly am."

"That is why I asked you to come home," Prince Oban whispered in his father's ear.

King Degnal suddenly leaned way back in order to take a good look at his son. He needed to see his face. Prince Oban slowly released his embrace of his father and stood erect. He immediately regretted what he had just uttered. Meanwhile, King Degnal replayed his son's words over and over again, and again in his hearing, 'That is why I asked you to come home… That is why I asked you to come home… That is why I asked you to come home… That is why I asked you to come home…'

"Everyone leave…" King Degnal said to no one in particular, still eyeing his son rather curiously.

Then he looked over at Commander Testlar and with a small gesture indicated that he needed the hall cleared out.

"My King," Commander Testlar said obeying the King's silent command while ushering everyone out through the main doors.

Moments later, the only two remaining in the hall were King Degnal and his son, Prince Oban. King Degnal sat still allowing the understanding of his son's words to sink in a little bit more before speaking.

"You know, I had a dream while I was away…" he began cautiously, "…A dream like none other…" he paused, "…Would you like to know what that dream was about?" King Degnal asked.

Prince Oban did not respond.

"…I thought I was going mad. I swore to the gods that there was someone in the chamber with me…" King Degnal said, "…In fact, I was convinced of it…"

King Degnal stared at his son. Prince Oban, who had been holding his breath, let it out rapidly with a sigh.

"…I believed that I was not alone…" King Degnal told him, "…Do you have any idea what that feels like; to feel as if you're being haunted…?"

King Degnal awaited an answer. None came.

"…Of course not. You are too young…" King Degnal said almost to himself, "…and yet, yet, I believe there are things…things that might seem impossible for some, but for others…well…?"

"Yes, my King father, impossible," Prince Oban responded.

"…and yet…" King Degnal said waving his arm out for his son to sit back down.

King Degnal then thought long and hard about the choices of his next words to his son. He didn't quite know how to inquire about the things he suspected. He finally decided to just ask knowing that the simplest way to obtain information always began with a question.

"Son?" King Degnal asked.

"Yes, King father," Prince Oban replied.

"Are you practicing the mystical, dark arts?" King Degnal asked sternly.

Prince Oban looked at his father and frowned.

"No, my King father. No," Prince Oban happily answered.

"I do not want your tutors to dabble in such things – ever!" King Degnal ordered.

"No, my King father…" Prince Oban assured his father, "…I don't even know about such things."

Prince Oban had a broad smile across his face. He looked like the young boy that he was again, instead of the boy filled with foreboding. He sat back in his chair and breathed a sigh of relief. King Degnal did the same. King Degnal knew that he might use the dark arts from time to time but didn't want his son mixed up in such a nasty business as magic, at least not at such a young age.

They sat quietly, both father and son, for several long moments, each enjoying the silence. Then King Degnal sat straight up again and sharply turned his head toward his son again.

"You...You said you asked me to come home...That is what you said..." King Degnal said now looking directly at his son, "...When did you ask me to come home?" King Degnal asked.

Prince Oban now squirmed in his seat. He didn't wish to answer his father. He didn't know why, but he felt that if he answered, his father would never look at him the same. More than anything else, he wanted his father to love him. He truly believed that if he told his father the truth, that his father would treat him differently and that would simply crush his young spirit.

With his father's eyes bearing down upon him, he finally lifted up his head and decided that he would be brave as he had read his father was at all times. After all, he was a Degnal, soon to be king of the kingdom. Surely, he could do this, answer his father truthfully.

"It was two moons ago, my King father…" Prince Oban answered.

King Degnal now shifted uncomfortably in his seat. Then he sunk back in his seat. It had been exactly two moons ago that he heard that voice in his head.

"H…How?" King Degnal asked his son.

"…I could hear your thoughts while you were in the village inn…" Prince Oban went on.

King Degnal looked at his son.

"…Then I just started talking to you," Prince Oban said succinctly.

King Degnal continued to stare at his son a while longer before leaning back on his throne and seriously contemplating every last word his son had just said. He truly didn't quite know what to think about any of it. His son, his own flesh and blood, had just told him that it was he who spoke to him in a dream, but now he knew it wasn't a dream. He would think it utter nonsense if he hadn't experienced it himself. He thought, 'What mystery is this?' His son, his very flesh and blood, had saved his Kingdom from ruin.

King Degnal turned to his son and said, "With this…gift of yours, you will be the greatest king who ever lived in the Great Lands, but you must promise me that you will never tell anyone of it."

Prince Oban now stared at his father, King Degnal, and simply said, "I promise."

CHAPTER 10. While King Degnal was still reflecting upon his narrow escape from the clutches of a villain in his Kingdom, King Runmari had already given orders to have his spies, together with their entire families, murdered on sight.

"Gather them together and dispose of them in front of one another..." he yelled, "...I want them to witness what I do to traitors!" King Runmari brutally barked.

His new mission in life was to find out who knew his plans of conquering Degnal Kingdom and more importantly, who told King Degnal. It never occurred to him that he had stealthily kept those secret desires to himself from the very beginning. Even his closest Generals and Lieutenants hadn't a clue. As far as his army was concerned, their King was just operating diplomatically with other realms. From the time he first heard of King Degnal's peculiar absence to the time that King Runmari decided to visit, he never let on to anyone what he wanted to do there.

Unfortunately, none of that mattered to King

Runmari. Lives would be lost at his hands for this egregious betrayal. He would rid his territory of the menace even if he had to go from village to village to personally find them. Ironically, now that he was having his spies killed, he might never get the answers he sought. No matter to him, for he was beyond reason, even more so than his usual disagreeable self. It was clear to everyone within his territories that, going forward, any opposition to his quest would be met with harsh retribution. No one was safe.

One of his forty children, his son, Mala, took to his bed at supper because he wasn't feeling well. King Runmari ordered one of his soldiers to drag him out of bed to the supper table and to place a hot poker on his son's tongue. Afterwards, Mala was forcefully fed an entire meal in front of the entire assembly for his amusement.

"Do not make a sound…" King Runmari shouted to Mala, "…else we will feed you seconds!"

Mala nodded his head, showing that he understood and held in his desire to even let out a whimper. Those present held in a gasp at the King's treatment of his very own son.

"Never deny the King's meal!" King Runmari barked at his son and his audience.

Around the table sat a handful of dignitaries and King Runmari's favorite wives, sixty of them in all. The rest of his one-hundred and two wives ate in the servants' quarters. Some said that the discarded wives were the happiest women within the kingdom. They were well taken care of without having to ever be in the company of the King.

King Runmari slobbered down his meal and gulped mouths full of several pitchers of beer. He was sufficiently drunk half-way through the night and belched and farted openly and repeatedly. Then he ordered all of his favorite wives to accompany him in his bed chamber for the night. The wives smiled uneasily, and when King Runmari stood to retire, they all followed him out of the super room.

His wives would try their hardest to please King Runmari even though there was no certainty that anything they attempted to do would calm him. King Runmari insisted that they bath him in the manner he received at the Degnal Kingdom. Since none of them accompanied him on his visit there, he had to instruct them every step of the way.

"Warm the water just so!" he shouted.

They heated the water hesitantly, all the while hoping the temperature was to his liking.

"I want it perfect!" he snapped.

They shuttered pouring the water while his servants disrobed him and submerged him uneasily into the tub. They were scared to death that he would be displeased. To their surprise, King Runmari nodded his approval at first, but far too quickly the water drew cold.

"It's frigid!" he yelled.

Then he reached his arm out and slapped the wife closest to him down to the floor. His other wives and the servants ran to the fire pit and heaved piping hot buckets of water from it to dump into the King's bath. When the heated water touched his skin, the King shrieked.

"Ahhhh!" he screamed, jumping up from the scalding water that had unfortunately burned his naked body.

He back-handed the two wives who poured water on him and they too landed on the floor looking semi-unconscious. For the blow he dealt them was powerful and hard. The remaining wives quickly sprung to his aid by wrapping a velvety soft robe around his smarting skin. As the cloth touched him, King Runmari screamed all the more.

"Ahhh....!" he yelled.

Then he punched another of his wives in the chin,

lifting her clean off her feet. She went sailing into a wall from the force of his mighty blow. The other two, who still had their hands on the robe, stood completely still awaiting what torture King Runmari would enact upon them. Thankfully, none came. Another of his wives quickly scooped some of the now cold bath water out of the tub and doused the King with it. The cooling water managed to sooth his aching body immediately. King Runmari grabbed that wife by the hair, snatched her up and swung her into his bed. She thought that he would strangle her to death, but instead he kissed her passionately.

That night and the ensuing days wore on miserably for the Runmari Kingdom. Public killings were becoming common-place in the territory. Even some of King Runmari's favorite wives fell victim to his anger when they were unable to please King Runmari in the manner he required at any given, random moment. He stabbed one in the stomach, because she walked a few steps ahead of him as they strolled around the palace pond. Another brought him a mug of beer without him asking for it. Her head was bashed into the stone floor. To make his point, he ordered his guards to leave their bodies where they landed as a warning to anyone who displeased him. After the incident with his son Mala, his other children hid in the servants' quarters for two entire winters. It was the only place King Runmari rarely ventured but they couldn't be sure that he never would.

It was three winters to the day of King Runmari's returning to his kingdom from the Degnal's, that the Runmarians received a reprieve from their King's wrath. It came from the most unlikely of sources. One cool fall day, King Runmari was visited by a resident of the Degnal Kingdom.

"He's in the courtyard, King Runmari," the first Lieutenant informed the King.

"Why the courtyard?" King Runmari asked curiously.

Normally, visitors were escorted into the palace in the reception hall. There, they would receive a warm welcome of a foot wash, a beverage and something to eat. It was unusual for someone to refuse such hospitality from such a long journey.

"He requested your immediate presence upon arrival, your grace," said the first Lieutenant.

"Run him through for his insolence…" King Runmari ordered, "…I am at no one's beck and call."

"Your Grace, of course…" the first Lieutenant agreed, and turned to exit, anxious to carry out the King's command.

Mere seconds later, the King rethought his orders.

"Wait," King Runmari said to his first Lieutenant.

The first Lieutenant turned back around and faced his King. King Runmari didn't wish to tell his first Lieutenant that he may have made a mistake.

"I wish to see this visitor before you plunge a dagger into him," King Runmari told his first Lieutenant.

The first Lieutenant about-faced and marched out, followed by King Runmari. The courtyard wasn't far off and before long they exited outside the palace onto the grounds. Unlike Degnal Palace's lush gardens, Runmari was filled with shrubs and hedges. Surrounding those were walkways of dark gravel and stones. It wasn't beautiful to look at, but it was neatly designed and structured.

The guest was standing a few arms lengths from King Runmari. King Runmari couldn't immediately see who it was because the guest had his back turned. Even this upset the King. He didn't like guests to begin with, but those who arrived unannounced might not live long enough to even see his displeasure. Fortunately, for this guest, King Runmari tried not to let his feelings show. Something within him bade that he be patient, and where he hadn't listened to anyone's advice lately, suddenly he decided to heed his own. His guest was fortunate indeed.

Once King Runmari and his first Lieutenant stood a couple of steps away from the guest, the gentleman turned and faced them. He hadn't heard anyone approaching because he was at an age where he was beginning to lose his sense of hearing. King Runmari was a little shocked by who had come to call. Nothing could have prepared him for this visit.

"King Runmari," the gentleman said while walking laboriously towards King Runmari, supporting himself with the use of a cane and bowing as low to the ground as he could manage.

King Runmari received the gentleman's gesture honorably by extending his hand and nodding respectfully towards him.

"I'm so glad that my first Lieutenant didn't carry out my order to have you killed, my friend, Burton," King Runmari chuckled waving for Burton to stand back up.

Burton lifted his head mechanically and eyed the first Lieutenant suspiciously. Then he smiled uncomfortably while touching his own neck to make sure it was still healthy without blemish.

While Advisor Burton was making sure his body was still in tack, King Runmari gestured for his army, including his first Lieutenant, to remove themselves from his presence. They quickly scattered from their King's sight, yet remained within proximity of his voice in case he needed them again. They would protect their King with their very lives should this guest prove to be an enemy.

King Runmari's guards watched closely as their King and Advisor Burton walked slowly away from them down the path around the palace. The irony of their King wanting to kill on sight the man he now seemed completely chummy with was not loss on them.

"Burton, this is certainly a surprise," King Runmari stated as a direct invitation for Burton to start talking.

Advisor Burton hesitated only briefly and smiled awkwardly. He was still reeling from the King's unnerving greeting.

King Runmari was shrewd and sensed his

uneasiness.

"About that comment earlier, we have been in the process of extinguishing traitors from our realm..." King Runmari chuckled, "...You understand?"

"Of course..." Advisor Burton replied emphatically, "...Of course."

Then they walked a bit further in silence, each sizing the other up before continuing their conversation.

"What brings you to Runmari territory? Did you miss me?" King Runmari asked, again with a chuckle.

He had to admit that he hadn't been quite himself lately and enjoyed this little diversion with his Degnal guest. He couldn't remember the last time he had a good laugh. He would flatly deny it to anyone else, but it warmed his heart to do so now.

"King Runmari, I come here ever so humbly with a small request," Advisor Burton said.

"...A request?" King Runmari asked.

King Runmari couldn't believe his luck. He was beginning to believe that this meeting might lead to another opportunity to somehow, and he didn't know how, but to somehow take Degnal Kingdom. At the very least, he thought that Burton might prove to be a good spy, especially

in light of the fact that he had killed off all his others.

"Why yes…" Advisor Burton said, "…It has become very disagreeable for me at the palace."

"Disagreeable?" King Runmari asked.

"Indeed," Advisor Burton replied.

"Indeed?" King Runmari asked becoming more and more intrigued with Advisor Burton.

"Why yes…" Burton began in a whisper.

As they strolled along, Advisor Burton started telling King Runmari about the goings on at the Degnal Kingdom in more detail. King Runmari soon found himself savoring every single word.

"…Of course you have not heard of the changes that have taken place at Degnal palace…" Burton continued.

"Of course," King Runmari said encouraging Burton to go on.

"…It's very unfortunate for all of us…" Burton exclaimed, "…We don't know what we're going to do. This has been our lives! It's just unheard of…"

Each word Burton spoke began to quickly lift King Runmari's darkened spirits.

"What? What is unheard of?" inquired King Runmari.

"…Why King Degnal's insistence of keeping us out of the daily business!" Burton nearly shouted.

"How so, Burton?" King Runmari asked, "How are you being kept from the talks?"

"That son of his, Prince Oban…" Burton said in a hush, "…He's the only one allowed in there with the King!"

King Runmari thought for a moment about what Burton had just told him. Could it be possible that the king was taking advice from a child? King Runmari laughed heartily. He too found the child engaging, but not so much as someone who could be considered as wise as a king.

"I see…" King Runmari said, trying to contain his laughter while outwardly agreeing with Burton's obviously appalled attitude over his King's behavior.

He couldn't believe his good fortune of having Burton come to him. His need for receiving juicy information was being graciously satisfied. Without any manipulation on his part, an opportunity was presenting itself right before his eyes. Suddenly, new hope for getting the Degnal Kingdom was coming into view. His old plan to seize it was giving way to an entirely new scheme with an unexpected twist. The real issue for King Runmari was if he could trust any of it.

"Burton, friend…" King Runmari began, "…Are you here looking for new employment?" King Runmari asked graciously.

Burton lifted his head and smiled. He didn't believe that he was so transparent, but he did like the fact that King Runmari was astute.

"I am long in winters and have long ago completed my personal duties to wife, family, and King. Relocating to more advantageous quarters, where my advisory skills are more appreciated, would be of benefit to someone deserving as such…as yourself, yes," Burton replied.

"I see," King Runmari nodded.

He thought, 'First, King Degnal abandons his kingdom, and now he's going mad!'

CHAPTER 11. Kena had always been of little to no significance to anybody. She was the lowliest of the low, the middle child of nine. As a young girl, her entire existence was to be seen, but rarely heard even in her own household - a small hut hidden behind an over brush of hedges, same as everyone else's of her station, in the peasants' quarters of the Degnal Palace. Her home was so far away from the palace that one would have to walk half a day to get to and fro.

Kena would never be asked what she thought, how she was faring; her opinion on any subject would never be entertained. Her parents, she and her siblings, were born into servitude; it was all they had ever known. They would never rise above that station for as long as their generations survived. That was Degnal Kingdom, the way of the times. She was by all accounts invisible.

Therefore, when Kena exclaimed an utterance loud enough to overshadow that of the Queen Mother in her very presence, she committed an unconscionable wrong.

The Queen Mother had just swallowed her last morsel of fish. Then she looked out at her servants as if she was contemplating sharing a thought with them, but then she decided against it. Instead, she sat erect and allowed her dining servant to delicately wipe crumbs from her lips. A long stretch of silence followed.

It was commonly known, but never ever discussed, that the Queen Mother had not quite been herself since the disappearance of her daughter, Asha. She had become seemingly a bit unstable. No one, including the King, wished to upset her increasingly unbalanced countenance. He instructed her servants to make sure she ate her regular meals and that she took at least one stroll outside daily. Unfortunately for them, she was blatantly uncommunicative regarding their requests and would glare at them harshly if they wanted to push an issue further. Her servants made adjustments by tip-toeing around her stealthily, speaking only in whispery hushes. Sometimes those days proved to be easier than others. Other times, the King would ask if his orders were being carried out and they would have to skillfully lie. Not only was their Queen Mother not eating at times, but she was not taking her walks either.

If the King discovered their lies, they would be

executed. If they displeased their Queen, they would be executed. The servants were becoming increasingly learned on how to tremble with fear while continuing to do their jobs. This day was no different, except the source of their tension was coming from one of their own – Kena.

The Queen cleared her throat and looked directly at Kena. Kena quickly lowered her head and prayed to every god she could think of; the sun, the moon, the stars, the wind, the morning, and the night. She was sure she had forgotten one and that that would be her downfall. She couldn't help but think how odd her life had been. Here she was experiencing the happiest day of her life, coupled with the saddest. If only she could have kept her joy to herself as she had always done in the past.

"Kena…" Queen Mother called and Kena took one measured step forward.

The entire chamber came to a complete standstill. Of course, Queen Mother knew who Kena was, after all she was Asha's constant aide, servant and chaperone. Yet no one had ever heard the Queen address her directly.

"… 'es, '…een," Kena finally managed, barely able to stand.

The Queen always took her time, but with this order,

she was particularly inert. Everyone present stood at attention neither looking to the left or the right. An order was about to be given and it might be to have poor Kena executed for insubordination.

"…Do go and find her for me…" the Queen said, without verifying whether Kena heard or understood her meaning.

Kena hesitated only a moment before she quickly turned on her heels and sprang from the chamber with all haste. Only when she was clear from the chamber, the servants, the guards, and especially from the Queen, did she begin to breathe again. She quickly and quietly thanked all the gods. She was grateful that they had spared her this time. Now that she knew her life wasn't in danger, a grin formed upon her face, so wide that she couldn't contain it, for the Queen had confirmed a suspicion that Kena had been grabbling with all night.

Her heart beat manically as she walked down the corridors of the palace and rounded the corner heading towards the Chamber of Agreement. Kena felt a tinge of fear, not wanting to relive memories of the last time she was before these doors with Princess Asha. To her surprise, as she approached the guards lowered their arms.

"…The Queen…" Kena said fretfully, too frazzled to repeat the Queen's order.

Suddenly, the Chamber of Agreement doors opened and Kena was escorted in. As the guards marched her in she felt nervous seeing the King's Advisor and military Commanders present. Then she looked forward and smiled with delight. At first she thought that her eyes were deceiving her, but no, Princess Asha was sitting with her father, King Degnal.

She quickly bowed before the King and the Princess, but her heart was all a flutter with the sheer joy she felt at Asha's return. Then before she knew it, she was practically lifted off her feet.

"Kena!" Asha screamed, hugging Kena warmly and kissing her on both cheeks.

They had never done this before, but they were always more than just servant and mistress, they were deadly close friends. Kena cried tears of joy and couldn't stop smiling at how much she had missed her mistress, the girl that she would have given her life for in any circumstance.

"I wish I were there and could have protected you, Princess. If only I were there…" Kena moaned.

"Kena, there was nothing you could have done. You would have been killed," Asha told her bluntly, "Then what? I would have lost you."

Princess Asha gently wiped the tears from Kena's face and brought her into a standing position. Kena straightened up and presented herself once more as Asha's servant. Princess Asha smiled and turned back around to face her father, King Degnal.

"I was just telling my King Father all about my harrowing experience," Asha said to both Kena and the King.

"Yes…how you escaped?" King Degnal asked as if he wanted more explicit details of his daughter's story.

King Degnal was already plotting his revenge and didn't wish to leave a single villain out of the nasty scheme he had planned for them, but Princess Asha didn't answer her father right away. Instead she strolled over to her little brother, Prince Oban, who was also present.

"You must be many winters now, my brother?" Princess Asha asked.

"Yes," Oban answered, "I am nearly eight," he replied.

"I see…" Princess Asha said.

"The same age as you when…" Prince Oban started.

"Yes…" Princess Asha said finishing his sentence, "…I can't believe how long it has been. You were just born," she smiled, remembering how hideous she thought he was then, but no more.

"I've grown a great deal since then," Prince Oban said proudly.

"Yes, you have…" Princess Asha told him, "…I cannot tell you what I considered we do with you upon your arrival…" she laughed, "…Let's just say, you are not as you were that day," Princess Asha said with a polite laugh.

Prince Oban did not join her in laughter, but instead narrowed his eyes upon her and stared.

"None of us are," he offered equally politely.

Princess Asha abruptly stopped laughing and turned once more to her father. She no longer wished to converse with her little brother. She got the impression that he was reading her mind. The eerie part was that she could have sworn that it wasn't just her imagination.

"My King Father, I'd like to lie down now. Can we continue this later?" Princess Asha asked.

King Degnal came down from his throne and hugged his daughter warmly.

"Of course…" King Degnal said, caressing his daughter and pulling her close, "…Of course."

He could barely release her from his arms. He missed her so terribly that if he held her any longer he would have sobbed uncontrollably. So, he waved his hand up and moments later no less than twelve heavily armed guards rushed to his side. When King Degnal returned to his throne, the guards surrounded Princess Asha like a human fortress. Princess Asha wanted to protest, but knew her father wouldn't hear of it.

She exited the Chamber of Agreement with her army and a very happy Kena following closely behind. Kena never told Princess Asha that her mother requested an audience with her. She didn't remember. She knew that it wouldn't matter now anyway. Now that Princess Asha was back in the palace, Kena's life would return to normal. She would answer to one mistress and one mistress only, her beloved Princess Asha.

The guards escorted the Princess to her bed chamber and insisted on at least three going inside to check on things first. They were ordered to make sure that no one else was in there this time. Princess Asha stood aside and waited patiently while the guards entered and searched every inch of the chamber thoroughly. Only after their investigation was completed were Princess Asha, her servants and Kena allowed inside.

To her dismay, her door would no longer be completely closed either. The guards left it ajar and stood with their backs to it in order to give her some modicum of privacy. It was becoming clear to Princess Asha that her father intended for her to be a prisoner in the palace and under armed guard indefinitely. She really couldn't blame him for his concern. She knew that possibly everyone in the Degnal Kingdom thought the same way– all save her.

Asha's servants were extremely overjoyed to bath and dress their Princess that evening. They were overwhelmed and beaming with pride for the good fortune of their King, believing that his royal divinity had somehow returned the Princess to the kingdom without a scratch upon her. Although the servants prayed for their King and Queen and for Princess Asha's safe return, none among them believed they'd ever see her again.

"Princess Asha, we are so happy of your return," one servant told her.

The rest smiled. Then each managed to give her a small treat in the best way they knew how. One brought her a tiny melon cut in rounded pieces the way she liked it. Another placed lavender in her bath water. Another warmed her bed so that she wouldn't experience a chill upon entering the blankets. Still others surrounded her adorningly and gazed upon her affectionately unable to pull themselves away. She was striking. Each was enamored with how well she looked. For them, she had grown up magically. Last they saw her, she was the young princess running around the palace daily and riding her giant horse throughout the kingdom, but she was a woman now, and one of great beauty and poise.

Princess Asha tried to receive the gifts graciously, but she was beginning to feel uncomfortable with so much attention given her.

"You may all leave now," she told them as gently as she could muster, but her words still came out sharply and curt.

She was feeling genuinely grateful toward them, but in equal measure she just wanted to be left alone to contend with her own thoughts. It had been ages since she had been in her own chamber, and thankfully for Kena, everything was exactly as she had left it. She was never fond of dolls, but the two that were given to her as gifts were right beside her bed, just as she remembered.

A portrait of the King and Queen with her beside them hung on the wall adjacent to the bed. She had always enjoyed looking at it, especially as an only child. She had thought about it often during her long absence and of how much it meant to her, of how much she missed her parents. She gazed at the images and remembered how happy she was then, just the three of them living out their royal lives in the most magnificent place she had ever known, Degnal Kingdom. She refused to mull over the vexing implication of the new addition to her family. She decided to deal with that at the new sun. 'Prince Oban,' she thought with a sigh. Suddenly, she grew tired.

Seeing her little brother again reminded her of his dramatic entrance into her quiet little world there at the Degnal Palace and her journey into obscurity. Only she alone knew the truth of what part her brother played as to why she was taken in the first place. She tried not to let that little fact ruin her return. No one could ever know how much she resented her brother, though one day she vowed to show him the consequences of his involvement. In her mind, he was responsible for her troubles, because he took her out of her rightful position in the Degnal legacy.

"Are you quite settled in for the night, Princess?" Kena asked her.

She was the only one allowed to remain with Princess Asha. They both knew that neither wanted to leave the other. Kena prepared to stay the night by dusting off a few mats that were strewn on the floor. As far as she was concerned, she would never leave her side again. She hoped beyond reason that she would never, ever have to.

"I'm very fine, Kena..." Princess Asha replied, "...Will you sing to me?" she asked.

Kena began to hum sweetly. The melody brought a tear to Asha's face. Of all the people in the Degnal Kingdom, she knew that she missed Kena the most. Kena was her confidant, her playmate and most of all, her only friend.

"You know...don't you?" Princess Asha suddenly asked Kena in a measured tone.

Kena stopped humming, turned around and looked directly at Princess Asha. She hesitated in responding. She didn't wish to anger Princess Asha in any way. She feared being separated from her again, especially for something she said. She took a deep breath.

"…We haven't any secrets…" Princess Asha said, reassuring Kena that she could speak freely.

Kena nodded her head and scrunched up her lips.

"How far along are you, Princess?" Kena asked in a hushed tone.

Princess Asha sat upon her bed. Suddenly, she was even more exhausted. Without answering Kena directly, Princess Asha said, "No one can know." Kena lowered her head and nodded again and this time with a tiny smile.

CHAPTER 12. The palace was quiet. All were still abed save Princess Asha and Kena. They arose early that morning. Things had greatly changed between them since Princess Asha's return. Normally, they'd be fast asleep before dawn, but that was then.

Nowadays, to their disappointment, they could no longer run throughout the palace like two youthful playmates. At present, Princess Asha had to participate in a rigorous schedule of royal related activities. Apparently, princesses had required duties. The Queen Mother would request her presence more often than not for meetings with other women of prominence throughout the Kingdom. Princess Asha began to realize that sitting amongst these types of women was what young ladies did for sport. She'd rather be out riding her horse, but that was only allowed on special occasions and always side saddle. They both had to grow up, Princess Asha and Kena. Unfortunately, Kena would be more servant-like and Asha would be more of a princess.

Dew was still sitting on the grass as they made their way across the palace grounds. The sun had yet risen. Their feet were sopping wet making it difficult for them to get down the mounds that led to their destination. Kena almost slid the whole way.

"I'm supposed to be helping you," Kena said in a sleepy chuckle.

Seeing Kena slip and slide, made Princess Asha more cautious with her footing.

"Let me slow down…" Princess Asha said, "…You do the same."

Kena followed suit and now measured each step as they traversed further through the meadow. The two of them were heading to the dress maker's hut. Kena had sent word via a chambermaid that Princess Asha was in need of new garments and, most importantly, she would like to be fitted for them before first light. Aside from the appointment time, this wasn't an unusual request.

When they finally arrived, they found the dressmaker already up with a kettle placed on the fire in preparation for her guests. Amma Khan was her name. No one knew her real age, but she had been in the Degnal employ for at least two kings, King Degnal and his father, King Dirk. She was the official royal palace seamstress and although everyone celebrated her creations, the King chose to keep her hidden from view. His reasoning in part was because she wasn't much to look at, with her shrunken back, woolly coarse hair and no teeth what-so-ever in her mouth. Traditionally, a palace seamstress would have an entire wing in the palace, an area dedicated to producing wardrobes, costumes and such, not a hut in the servants' section afar off from the palace proper.

No matter this distinction in her residence, Amma Khan was pleasant and cheerful. As soon as she saw the Princess, she bowed low to the ground and stayed there until she was asked to stand back up. She did so gracefully despite the hump in her back. Kena nearly laughed at the sight of it. She could have sworn it was smaller when last they saw each other. Princess Asha seemed not to notice. She was preoccupied elsewhere.

"Sit, my lady. I'll fetch you some tea," mumbled Amma Khan.

"Thank you," Princess Asha replied, plopping down in a comfy chair.

Amma Khan used the fabric of her skirt to lift the

piping hot kettle. She poured water into three preset mugs and handed one to Princess Asha, one to Kena, and grabbed the last one for herself.

Both Princess Asha and Kena looked curiously into their mugs and then at each other. Neither understood why Amma Khan was calling it tea when there weren't any tea leaves on the surface of the brew.

"Taste!" Amma Khan shouted gently.

Princess Asha and Kena lifted their mugs and sipped the content within carefully. It was the hottest liquid they'd ever tasted, but it didn't burn their tongues. It had the oddest texture to it. The consistency of the drink was like maple, yet the quality was smooth, rich and light. Plus, it was absolutely delicious! Princess Asha and Kena lifted their heads from the mugs, looked across at each other again and smiled.

"It's the best brew in the Great Lands…" Amma Khan said proudly, "…I blend it myself."

Kena gulped hers down rapidly and then sat placidly with her eyes gently closed and her mouth still tingling from the tea.

"Would you like some more?" Amma Khan asked Kena.

Kena immediately shook her head yes and thrust her mug forward to Amma Khan. They both giggled as Princess Asha did the same. Amma Khan took both mugs and poured them both some more. When she turned to give them the mugs, Princess Asha and Kena were standing behind her ready to receive the drink.

"Sip slowly this time, ladies…" Amma Khan said, "…I don't have enough for another mug."

Princess Asha and Kena did as they were told, savoring every delightful drop.

Then the ladies sat in blissful silence enjoying this early morning delight. Soon, it was as if the three didn't have a care in the world. They reclined in their seats, feeling peaceful and calm. Princess Asha and Kena had almost forgotten why they had come to see the seamstress. Eventually Amma Khan placed a brick of bread before them and ripped pieces off for each. Princess Asha and Kena couldn't wait to taste it. When they did, they each thought that even the baked goods were delicious. Amma Khan just smiled at them both knowing that although others saw her life as ordinary, she knew its unique beauty. When items were thrown away from the palace, Amma Khan gathered them up. She was able to blend and mix what was discarded and make it into the equivalent of a royal recipe. She smiled again realizing that she couldn't tell a soul that everything she ate was once garbage. That was her secret.

"Princess Asha, it is an honor to have you back with us," Amma Khan said with a smile.

With that comment, both Princess Asha and Kena were jarred back to reality. Princess Asha pulled herself erect in her seat and lowered her head. She was thinking of all the impossibilities that awaited her next decisions. She could lose everything if she didn't apply extremely well thought out, cunning plans.

She fidgeted with her hair in contemplation a moment, trying to find the exact words to say to Amma Khan. She needed Amma Khan and she didn't want to reveal too much without knowing for sure that Amman Khan would be as loyal to a Princess as she was to a King.

"How many moons along are you, my Princess?" Amma Khan asked with sensitivity and tact.

Princess Asha sat stoically knowing that any gesture would give her away. Kena tried not to move at all, although she wanted to glance over at Princess Asha badly.

"Amma Khan, what do you mean?" Princess Asha

innocently asked her.

"I'm elderly, broken and hunched, but I'm not blind," Amma Khan told her.

"I will not be spoken to like this!" Princess Asha said feigning indignation and standing up to leave.

"I'm excellent at keeping secrets…" Amma Khan said in a non-threatening, sing-songy manner.

Princess Asha lowered herself back into her seat. Then she slumped upon it as if standing completely wore her out.

"You cannot speak to the Princess in any manner you please," barked Kena, who then ran to Princess Asha's side.

"…I can help…" Amma Khan told them both and at that they turned and listened, "…I'm an old woman with much wisdom…" she continued matter-of-factly.

Princess Asha waved Kena away and leaned forward to speak with Amma Khan directly.

"Help?" Princess Asha asked in a way that let Amma Khan know that she had her full attention.

"Yes. Help…" Amma Khan said, "…I'm an excellent seamstress…" she smiled, showing fleshy gums, "…That is why you came to me, correct?"

Princess Asha slumped back in the seat again and sighed.

"Does it show?" Princess Asha asked in a whisper.

She realized at that precise moment that she had been afraid of saying it out loud, feeling that if she had, it would make her predicament that much worst.

"Not to the average person, no…" Amma Khan told her assuredly.

Princess Asha sat back feeling a bit more at ease.

"…I have seen it all, naturally, so of course I see it…but even midwives wouldn't be able to tell this about you yet…but eventually, of course, they will…" Amma Khan said.

Princess Asha glared at Amma Khan.

"They will, won't they?" Princess Asha said in a small panic.

"…Unless…" Amma Khan started.

"Unless what?" Kena asked.

Princess Asha glanced at Kena for silence.

"Unless what, Amma Khan? Unless what?" Princess Asha anxiously asked.

"…Unless, we fool them," Amma Khan said cryptically.

"Fool them," Kena mouthed doubtfully.

"Fool them," Princess Asha repeated with full recognition of what Amma Khan was proposing.

"Look, you came here because, upon your return to the palace, you grew up in every sense of the word..." she smiled, "...and now need clothes that fit, right?" She paused, "...Well, I can make them fit that too, without anyone being the wiser..." Amma Khan said standing and gesturing toward Princess Asha's midsection, "...I've done it before and I can do it again."

Princess Asha felt almost relieved, though she did wonder what Amma Khan meant by, '...I've done it before.' Princess Asha never considered that there might be a way out of her predicament.

Eventually, Kena caught on too and was extremely happy for her mistress, though she couldn't imagine how something like that could be hidden with cloth. Women with-child usually grew bigger and bigger as the baby grew bigger inside. She doubted very strongly that even a seamstress as good as Amma Khan could hide that.

"Amma Khan, please tell me what you want me to do and I'll do it," Princess Asha told her.

"Well, there will be a time when you must take an

extended journey away from the palace…" Amma Khan mentioned casually, "…of course."

Princess Asha knew full well the meaning and implications of those words. She couldn't very well remain in the palace indefinitely. She would begin to show and no clever garment would protect her from nature, nor from her father, the King.

Kena wanted to reach out to her and comfort her, but decided to join her instead in worrying in silence about their future. After all, she would be deemed an accomplice in this deceit should they be found out. They sat quietly, each staring into the hut solemnly.

Amma Khan knew their thoughts and their troubles. She stood up and made her way over to a secluded section of her home. She thereupon began to carefully unravel a drawstring that was tied around a heavy woolen curtain.

"This way, Princess…" Amma Khan motioned for Princess Asha to follow her, "…We need to get you properly fitted."

Princess Asha stood up and joined Amma Khan behind the curtain, while Kena continued to sit and worry alone.

CHAPTER 13.

"So, do we have an agreement?" King Runmari asked a rather uncertain Advisor Burton, who stood rigidly with his fingers arranged in a prayer pose touching his lips.

Advisor Burton didn't wish to let it show, but he felt ill at ease with the proposal King Runmari had just presented to him. In fact, he was beginning to feel sorry that he had ever ventured so far from home. It was assuredly uncharacteristic of him to run off as if he was still in his youth. Back then, he was employed as one of Degnal Palace's Royal Messengers. He was but a boy then. He'd run hither to and fro with the quickness of a gazelle. Now, having seen so many winters, he couldn't even arise from bed without the assistance of a stick. Then, he was constantly being praised for his swiftness, accuracy, and cunning. He rose up the ranks quickly and easily, sooner than most. Finally, he was rewarded for his intellect with a position of prominence in the Kingdom and remained there most of his adult life, having started before marrying age.

He was so needed, trusted, and respected, his wedding day was held during midday meal while he continued to conduct his service to the King.

That is why standing before King Runmari presently astonished him of his own naivety. This entire enterprise seemed so simple to him in its inception. He'd just leave the palace and go elsewhere-simple. He was no longer needed at Degnal Palace. His King had his new trusted advisor – his peevish son, Oban. He'd just go where he was needed, start afresh. He'd embark on an entirely new kingdom, Runmari Kingdom. He'd regale them with all of his proven knowledge and tried and true wisdom.

In his most generous opinion, the place was a shambles compared to Degnal. The opulence of Degnal made Runmari seem like a horse stable, a somewhat organized, chaotic one, but nonetheless, a place for animals. Beer drinking on the roads was permitted and upon Burton's arrival, he could barely stomach the smell of vomit throughout. He told himself that if he stayed, that would be the first thing he changed. He'd have the place smelling of jasmine and lilac before the first full moon. He'd also overhaul the kitchen staff. He only ate the mutton out of politeness. It was tougher than armor and tasted of shoe lacquer. Advisor Burton was tempted to ask the royal cook if that was the main ingredient. Though, with everyone else eating and enjoying it, he could hardly protest.

Besides, worse than all of that was the décor of the depressing palace. He didn't even want to think about how much help that troubled department needed. He would insist on bringing the Degnal Royal Decorators there for a visit, during which they would tear down Runmari's Palace and start from scratch. In his estimation, one would have to build the entire structure over from the ground up. Firstly, they would have to add windows. King Runmari was so paranoid that he built all of his structures without windows. Instead there were small slits in the walls that were too tiny for someone to crawl through, but big enough for arrows to be drawn out. The entire palace looked and felt as if it were a fort. Advisor Burton already missed the majestic views of the Degnal Kingdom seen from the Degnal Palace windows. He hadn't realized how light and airy it was until he had ventured to Runmari's Palace which felt more like a tomb.

"Your answer?" asked King Runmari of his guest.

Advisor Burton knew in his very soul that he couldn't say anything other than yes. In his brief visit there to the Runmari Palace, he had seen three men killed right in front of him, each in ways and for reasons that shouldn't have warranted death. Plus, there were several dead bodies bound and posted throughout the trail on his way in. Why he hadn't noticed the brutality of King Runmari at Degnal now troubled and amazed him. He was usually such a good judge of character. That used to be his stock and trade - to discern the nature of individuals for his King. Now, he knew with absolute certainty that he was standing before a brutal butcher.

"You can count on me," Advisor Burton answered, and with that, so sealed his fate to a most certain swift and gruesome death.

The only question in his mind was, would it be done by King Runmari or King Degnal?

He had plenty of time to mull over that question on the way back to Degnal Kingdom, and mull it over he did. In fact, it plagued him so that he scarcely wished to breath. Among other troubling things, King Runmari insisted on him traveling in style and spared no expense. An army of Runmari guards flanked Advisor Burton's dazzling carriage, riding in perfect formation the entire way. Advisor Burton would have been impressed had he not been continually reminded that they were Runmari guards. He tried desperately to convince King Runmari that he didn't need an armed escort back to Degnal, but King Runmari wouldn't hear of it. King Runmari wanted King Degnal to see how well he kept one of his trusted Advisors. He thought that King Degnal would think it the works of a good King to return a man of service back to another King unharmed and well cared for.

Advisor Burton knew that King Degnal would think exactly the opposite. For Advisor Burton hadn't told King Degnal the truth at his departure. He informed King Degnal that he would like to vacation outside of the Degnal Kingdom territory. He had never lied to anyone before let alone a king, his King! His hands shook and he felt nauseated, but he lied through his teeth to someone who trusted him for his entire life. That very day he felt elated and mortified at the same time. He leaped home and packed his garments as if he were truly voyaging. He was happy in his pretense. At the exact same time, he also felt remorseful and saddened by the betrayal he had commented to his King. It wasn't until he entered Runmari Kingdom that he realized he could be court marshaled and hung as a traitor. That wasn't the grand finale he had envisioned for his life. Again, he couldn't believe his naivety. His plan was a foolish one and now he could do nothing but follow it all the way through to its bitter, tragic end.

Advisor Burton was summoned to the Degnal Palace the moment he entered its gates. Runmari's guards, of course, were sent back to their home immediately. Advisor Burton tried at no avail to relieve them of their duties as soon as they arrived at the last village before the palace. They didn't answer him, but instead repeatedly stated their allegiance to King Runmari.

"Honor to King Runmari! Long live King Runmari!" they shouted.

Advisor Burton wasn't a violent man normally. So his desire to plunge a dagger into each one of them came as a surprise even to him. His anxiety at having a meeting with King Degnal upon being carted into Degnal territory chauffeured by King Runmari's men, mounted into sheer and utter panic. He found himself praying that whatever the punishment bestowed upon him that it would be brief.

"Welcome back, Burton," King Degnal told him as he entered into the Chamber of Allegiance. 'Why of all the chambers, are we to meet here?' thought Advisor Burton woefully. It was his least favorite room in the Palace. It was in this room that King Degnal met with foreign nations to pledge an alliance. Those who agreed with King Degnal were given a document to sign using their blood. Those who opposed King Degnal were most times relieved of their lives. Blood stain removal was actually a challenge for the royal help causing King Degnal to have a designated spot in which to dispose of the bodies. He'd direct his victim into the center of the room and would surround them with guards so they couldn't escape their fate. This day Advisor Burton was asked to stand on that very same spot. It didn't comfort him that only one guard stood beside him. He knew that it wouldn't take but one to do him in. If he were still one of King Degnal's trusted advisors, he would have advised the King to do this exact same thing.

"Thank you, my King," mouthed a very shaky Advisor Burton.

King Degnal took his time in asking, "Am I?" Advisor Burton knew his meaning and immediately answered, "Of course, my King." King Degnal grinned and clasped hands together in thought. Advisor Burton had seen his King do this very same gesture before nodding to the guards to do away with people. Advisor Burton closed his eyes and awaited the jab of the sword. None came. Instead King Degnal came toward Advisor Burton and took his hand.

"So, you traveled to Runmari Kingdom?" asked King Degnal in a friendly manner.

Advisor Burton nodded, but said nothing. He wasn't sure if the tone of his King was cordial or menacing. He was completely taken off guard.

"How is the King?" asked King Degnal.

"Fine, my King," Advisor Burton told him, emphasizing 'my King.'

"Is he now?" asked King Degnal.

"Yes, he is…my King," Advisor Burton said almost as a question.

"Oh, I'm asking because when last we saw him he was a bit shaken. You remember?" asked King Degnal.

Advisor Burton seemed a bit shaken himself. King Degnal removed Advisor Burton's hand and stared at him.

"As I recall, King Runmari wished to take a good look at our Kingdom…" King Degnal said, now walking back to his throne, "…I do wonder why he came all this way out of curiosity…Do you have any ideas?" King Degnal asked rhetorically.

King Degnal now stared at Advisor Burton with his head lowered and his eyes narrowed on him pointedly. Burton wanted to tell the guard to just get this entire business over with. He was mortified. How had his intellect brought him to this conclusion? He was in a worst state than he was before he left Degnal Kingdom.

"My King…" Advisor Burton began.

"Yes!" King Degnal barked startling Burton to near collapse.

"…You are a wise King…" Advisor Burton told him, "…I'm at your mercy, my King."

It truly was all he could say now that he had unwittingly placed himself in this ungodly position. Instead of being at Degnal Palace as nothing more than a footstool, he was now front and center positively the most hated man in the palace, all because he didn't like the King's attention to his own son. He had been a fool, an old fool.

"Yes, my old friend, you are," King Degnal said and in a moment, the guard standing beside Advisor Burton unlatched his sword and placed the blade upon Burton's neck. Burton stood rigidly and closed his eyes.

"I wish that it didn't come to this, Burton," King

Degnal said genuinely.

"I too wish the same, my King," Advisor Burton said equally genuinely.

"Before we commence with this ugly business, what was the nature of your conversation with King Runmari?" asked King Degnal.

The blade wasn't lowered with this question. Even as Advisor Burton breathed, he could feel the cold steel upon his flesh.

"A marriage…" Advisor Burton told him.

At that, King Degnal waved and the guard removed the sword from Burton's neck.

"Go on," King Degnal said.

"King Runmari would like to propose an alliance with you King Degnal, one of marriage," Advisor Burton said.

"Marriage?" asked King Degnal in contemplation of the suggestion.

He hadn't thought of such. He did know from his sources that King Runmari had no lack of children while he had but two. He would gain so much from a union of this nature. He knew that King Runmari was an enemy, and therefore one to watch. What better way to keep an eye on him, than to befriend him. There would always be the possibility of treachery, but neither would win territory easily with such an alliance. There would be so much for each to lose in a full-fledged war.

Advisor Burton swiftly recognized the shift in King Degnal's demeanor and seized the opportunity to tell yet another lie.

"I couldn't very well tell the King that I was going to negotiate on his behalf at the onset..." Advisor Burton said, "...you understand?"

"Yes. Yes. Quite," King Degnal agreed.

Advisor Burton sighed inside with relief at King Degnal's new posture. He sat easily upon his throne looking thoughtful now. Advisor Burton began to relax too until he reached up and touched his neck. There was an indentation there from the guard's sword.

"I wanted to tell you my King, but of late you have been preoccupied with the rearing of the Prince, of course," Advisor Burton threw in for good measure.

Now that he had told his second lie to the King, he was less apprehensive of doing so. To his shame, it almost felt natural.

"There is nothing more important than taking the

tyke under your wing and raising him up to be king," Advisor Burton added with a flourish.

At the mentioning of Prince Oban, King Degnal's countenance was completely changed. He loved the boy so that even thinking of him brought the King joy. Advisor Burton couldn't believe his luck in all this. Moments ago he desired death, only to now be back in the King's good graces. He took a step out of the center of the chamber toward the King, only to be abruptly stopped by the guard again with a sword to his throat.

"My King!" Burton shouted.

"Not so fast, my dear Advisor Burton," King Degnal said sternly.

Burton's heart sank.

"You might think me stupid…" King Degnal said, stepping down from his throne and walking slowly toward Advisor Burton.

"I would never, my King," Advisor Burton said through tears.

"…You would be wrong to assume that – ever!" King Degnal shouted, "…You asked for employment from King Runmari…" he said, and waited to see Advisor Burton's reaction.

Advisor Burton's eyes widened in panic, giving King Degnal the necessary confirmation he needed.

"My King?" Advisor Burton asked, all the while wondering how King Degnal could have possibly known.

"...You fool!" King Degnal shouted at him, "...Why would a killer such as King Runmari wish to employ a weakling like you?" he asked, "...You took your chances with a murderer and how well did that fare?" he asked and with that gave the order to have Advisor Burton executed.

The King's guard slashed Burton's throat with quick precision, then let the limp body drop to the floor. Advisor Burton still had a look of sheer panic across his face, all the while wondering with his last breath how the King knew what was discussed at a private meeting held between him and King Runmari.

CHAPTER 14. That very next day, a royal funeral was held in honor of Advisor Burton, despite Commander Testlar's vehement protest against it. The word treason was never mentioned, at King Degnal's command. In fact, the ceremony was quite the contrary. Advisor Burton was given a respectful send off, one befitting those of whom the King dearly loved.

The Degnal people believed that life did not end with death, but continued on to another, even greater realm. Traditionally, those related to the royal family would undergo a series of dynamic processes in which their life force would eventually ascend to the level of royalty even in the next life.

With that philosophy, Advisor Burton was painstakingly and ritualistically prepared for his journey to the other side. As he served the royal family in life, his service would continue in the afterlife. Advisor Burton was given specific burial rites that would ensure that he would.

An improper burial was reserved for those who

disobeyed their King. In those cases the deceased would be doomed to everlasting punishment and torture where they were beaten and expelled from their ancestors in the afterlife, wandering ghost without anchor. To be cut off from one's ancestors in death was the nearest equivalent to hell for the Degnal people. Those types of burials were only set aside for the most egregiously, wicked offenders. For those crimes and serious misdeeds, bodies would be chopped up first, and then burned, with remains fed to hyenas and what was left would be scattered throughout the territory so that the spirit could not somehow reassemble and haunt those who were still in the land of the living.

Although King Degnal no longer trusted Advisor Burton, he did not wish to have his Advisor's spirit roaming freely about and able to invade his thoughts with ghostly reminders of how he killed him. No, King Degnal was too shrewd for that and preferred Advisor Burton to resume the role of his servant especially in his next life. That way, King Degnal would for all eternity keep his foot firmly pressed upon his neck.

King Degnal smiled wickedly, looking forward to doing just that to Burton. 'Traitor,' King Degnal thought even while conveying his deepest sympathies to his remaining Royal Advisors and to Burton's family.

King Degnal made sure that the official word on Advisor Burton's death was that King Runmari committed it. With the King's pronouncement on the matter, now everyone in the Degnal Kingdom had a new enemy to occupy themselves with and pretty soon all terrible occurrences were linked somehow to King Runmari. Even those who witnessed Advisor Burton entering Degnal Palace very much alive, and never exiting, supposed that maybe they were imagining what they saw.

"I will send my best men to the Runmari territory to inquire as to why our dearly departed Advisor Burton was so brutally butchered. Swift justice will be carried out. I assure you…" King Degnal informed the very sorrowful Burton widow, "…Of course, you and your family will be taken care of forever by royal decree."

"You are so kind, my King…" the sobbing Burton widow cried, "…most kind and gracious, my King."

Then King Degnal stood with the widow and grieved with her openly and honestly, for he actually did have affection for the late Advisor Burton even with all that had transpired between them. In the immediate future it would plague him greatly how someone he had trusted, someone who was like a father to him, could betray him so overtly. As far as he could surmise there wasn't anything that he had done to Advisor Burton to trigger this behavior, although, he couldn't be completely sure about that fact. He doubted that he would ever be able to discover the actual cause of this blatant disloyalty. Advisor Burton had always acted in the interest of the kingdom and with total and undeniable respect for the King. King Degnal never had to question his allegiance on any issue at any time throughout their entire relationship. The only possible explanation King Degnal could find for this uncharacteristic disregard for him was that King Runmari had to have somehow bewitched him into deserting his King and his kingdom, his mission, his home. King Degnal would not rest until he had paid King Runmari back for his part in Advisor Burton's demise.

Princess Asha and Prince Oban joined their father, King Degnal, for a light supper after the services were held for Advisor Burton, together with the other Royal Advisors, Commander Testlar, and some of Degnal Kingdom's finest dignitaries and upper class citizens. Though the entire Palace and surrounding territories attended the ceremonies, only invited guests were allowed to dine with the King.

The Queen Mother retired to her bed chamber

explaining that grief for Advisor Burton had overtaken her.

"I need rest…" she said to King Degnal, "…The last thing he said to me was that he loved Deg…Deg…Deg…Deg…Degnal…" Queen Mother mouthed softly while exiting.

She had known Advisor Burton since she was a little girl and always regarded him as a close friend. She would miss him. She still couldn't believe that he was actually gone. Nor did she think she could bring herself to sit at a table and manage not to fall apart every time she glanced at his empty chair throughout the meal. She held back tears while being escorted to her bed chamber.

King Degnal noted the Queen Mother's swift departure with a tinge of indifference, for he knew the truth about his wife. He was well aware that she hadn't quite been herself since their daughter, Asha, was taken away from them. Even at Asha's return, Queen Mother still hadn't seemed to have recovered. And now, with Advisor Burton being lured away by a foreign kingdom and then murdered, well, this was enough to shatter her completely.

Certainly he was concerned with the thought of her taking her own life, but more so, he was worried of how that act would sully his image. This sullen attitude of hers was problematic for him. He was wary of having a wife who no longer regarded Degnal, the Kingdom that he reigned over, as a safe place. He decided to watch her more closely because of this, fearing that others would soon be swayed by her opinion. A King ruling over a people who lacked confidence in their King was a people who would soon rebel against him. He refused to be a casualty of his own people. He would have to do away with this current wife should that prove to be the case.

Lucky for Queen Mother, no one really noticed his wife's persistent melancholy. He hoped they never would. In the meantime he'd deal with the object of her distress. For it was his as well. Firstly, he'd take care of King Runmari. Then he would deal with the parties who took his daughter.

Unbeknownst to King Degnal that somber evening, his plans would have to wait. Unfortunately, a dark cloud was about to descend upon his kingdom, the likes of which he had never encountered.

Less than a day's ride away from the Degnal territory border rode the entire Kenneth army. Forty thousand warriors strong galloped on horseback steadfast towards their prey, equipped with archers, lancers, pick axes, knives and clubs. Though Kenneth had never been at war, each warrior was formidable in his own right, having been trained rigorously in all aspects of the art of war, killing, and mortal combat since their childhood. All were willing to die for their kingdom, and would do so without hesitation. Fighting for one's people was a philosophy that earmarked the Kenneth people. Truthfully, there wasn't anything finer in Kenneth than being a soldier. It was one of the noblest of professions.

Surely, they were fearsome warriors, but they would be fighting the Degnal army, who were equal in might, in weaponry and skill. In fact, the Degnal army was known throughout the Great Lands for their exceeding ferociousness in battle. Legend had it that one Degnal warrior could easily subdue ten powerful warriors. Plus, the Degnal army possessed an endless array of war victories and no defeats. They too groomed their young males to be proficient fighters; each breed to die for their King and kingdom as well.

War between these two great powers would be immense. The bloodshed would cripple both nations regardless of who became the victor.

Kenneth was well aware that they would be up against the most feared army of their day, but that didn't matter to them. Their mission was clear. They would avenge the culprits who committed crimes against their brethren. If they had to, they would make everyone pay. The warriors orders were simple - murder every male in the Degnal Kingdom, including its King.

"We shall finally remove that shadow of protection from around them," Elder Isoba shouted with a glint in his eyes.

"Aye!" roared the vast Kenneth army.

Kenneth would assure success in this task giving each Kenneth soldier the mystical potion to drink prepared by their Priest, Godlumthakathi. It would be their secret weapon, a distinct advantage over the Degnal army.

According to Priest Godlumthakathi, the Degnal army would be scared out of their wits at the sight of the Kenneth warriors marching toward them. The Priest told the Kenneth warriors that their enemy wouldn't have time to retreat, for they would be too frozen with fear to move. Godlumthakathi said that the army could then kill as many as they desired without retaliation. The Kenneth warriors were looking forward to this. They couldn't wait to see the looks of terror on the faces of the Degnal army.

With such a great guaranteed victory, Kenneth rode hard throughout the night and the day. They hadn't slept but drove forward without slowing down their pace or taking a break. Their mission was clear. They were going to annihilate Degnal Kingdom and wipe it from the face of the earth. Priest Godlumthakathi's elixir helped. Not only did the brew give them super human strength, it also made them feel tireless and invincible.

Before dawn they had already breached the further most corner of the Degnal territory, the sleepy village of Larson. Its citizens were abruptly awaken by Kenneth foot soldiers. All of the Larson men were killed; most while they yet slept. The women and children were spared, left to wail uncontrollably and forced to wait on and serve the Kenneth soldiers.

Of all the Larson inhabitants, only one managed to escape, a girl of nine winters named Chinaza. She rode off on her family's mule to the neighboring village of Kassel. Her soul purpose, to warn them of impending doom.

CHAPTER 15. There in Larson, Kenneth soldiers felt quite proud of their victory. Just as Priest Godlumthakathi said, the villagers shriveled in fear at the sight of them. For an army who had never been in battle before, they were astonished. Miraculously, they entered the village, simply walked up to the men and thrust their swords and spears into them. The Larson men didn't even run or resist them. Instead they stood frozen and panic-stricken, while the Kenneth army roamed from hut to hut encountering man after man with that same peculiar stance.

Then after eating and drinking their fill of Larson's beer and meat, the Kenneth army mounted their steeds and rode off savoring their triumph and longing for a similar experience with the next Degnal village. As they road onward, two Kenneth riders were dispatched to ride back and tell the Elders about their success.

Later, at sunrise, Kenneth soldiers approached Kassel village, eagerly longing to ascertain who the culprit was that committed the crime against their brethren. This would be a simple task. They'd find the men and women standing like statues at the sight of them, as they had before. They entered, but this time no one greeted them.

The Kenneth scouts were immediately called forth to answer for the whereabouts of the Degnal village people.

"We saw them here at first light, sir…" a scout told the ranking soldier, "…I don't know where they could have gone."

Kenneth's first ranking soldier, Talib, lowered his head in contemplation. He wondered, as did his fellow soldiers, how an entire village managed to clear out without a trace.

"Dismount and search!" Talib hesitantly shouted.

At once, the Kenneth army lowered themselves from their horses and began going from hut to hut in search of the Degnal people. Kassel was a thriving village with more than ten thousand souls, not including women and children. It was highly unlikely that they had ridden out of the village having heard that Kenneth was coming. Talib knew that a better explanation was that they were all in hiding.

Unfortunately, after a thorough search of the entire village, the Kenneth soldiers could not find a single resident.

Talib and his men were utterly baffled. They were also exceedingly disappointed that they wouldn't have an opportunity to settle the score with the Kassel men who assaulted their people.

"We will mount up and go to the next Degnal village!" Talib ordered, frustrated beyond measure with this outcome.

Then, without another word spoken, the Kenneth army mounted their steeds once more and followed Talib out of Kassel village. They were still bewildered by what took place, but now anxious to take their revenge out on the next unsuspecting Degnal village.

As soon as the Kenneth soldiers cleared the two mountains that stood a great distance away from Kassel village, a spray of dust suddenly filled the air outside the main road leading to Kassel's entrance. Then on that same spot, a patch of earth shifted slowly to one side and a hole began to appear. Out of it popped one of the Kassel village merchants, followed in quick succession by the entire village, including the young girl, Chinaza.

The villagers ran in every direction checking to make sure their homeland was completely free of all the

Kennethians. After which, the village broke out in celebration the likes of which were rarely seen, all the while congratulating Chinaza for her bravery in alerting them. Several guards had already been dispatched to warn the other villages and to notify the King.

Chinaza was the only one who emerged from the crevice sorrowful. She was saddened by the day's events, still reeling at the loss of her father and brothers and all the other men of her village the day before. She longed to travel back home and check on her mother and sisters. But the Kassel villagers wouldn't hear of it and insisted she stay and enjoy the festivities. They would make provisions for her to leave at the new sun.

The Kassel villagers enjoyed their feasting that entire evening with leftover bread, beef jerky and warm beer. They were overjoyed to have bested the fearsome giants of Kenneth especially since they hadn't needed to lift a finger to do so.

News of this nature spread quickly throughout the Degnal Kingdom and even the surrounding Kingdoms. It didn't take long before word made it back to Kenneth. The Elders sat solemnly worried about their army. None wished to speak on it, but all knew that their men were now vulnerable in addition to being the laughing stock of the Great Lands.

"How is this possible?" Elder Nafari queried to no one in particular.

Suddenly his worst nightmare was coming true.

"Did Priest Godlumthakathi's spell work or not?" Elder Sam asked the Elders.

No one answered Elder Sam's question, but pondered it instead. Each wondered what could have possibly gone wrong with such powerful magic and the best weaponry in the Great Lands.

"I'm afraid that we have been beaten by something even more dynamic than our greatest defense…" Elder Isoba said sadly, "…I never thought it possible."

"Neither did I," Elder Nafari agreed.

"Nor I," rang out throughout the assembly from the other Elders.

"What do we do now?" Elder Duna asked.

"And do we still have to pay Priest Godlumthakathi?" Elder Nafari asked in a shaky voice.

The Elders sat silently considering Elder Nafari's question. Priest Godlumthakathi warned them repeatedly of the consequences of using this particular spell. It was the most dangerous of all the spells. It required the highest price.

"One of us must tell him that it didn't work, of course," Elder Sam suggested.

"Who will do that?" Elder Duna asked indignantly.

He didn't want that Elder to be him. He felt, as they all had, that whoever approached Priest Godlumthakathi would be the one to be put to death.

"I will," Elder Isoba pronounced.

Elder Isoba wasn't trying to be brave. In fact, he was feeling quite the contrary. He thought that since all of this was his idea that he should be the one to stand up to the Priest.

"Are you sure?" asked Elder Nafari.

Elder Isoba simply nodded, 'yes.'

While the Kenneth Elders were discussing their predicament, King Degnal and Commander Testlar were summarizing theirs.

"Each village is safe and secure, my King," Commander Testlar announced.

"Excellent…" King Degnal told his Commander,

"…Excellent!"

The unique Degnal holes had been in existence since the times of King Degnal's father. His father enlisted skilled laborers to dig them and fashion their coverings in such a way so that they were undetectable to on-lookers. Since their erection, to King Degnal's recollection, they hadn't been used. There wasn't a need because Degnal had never been attacked before until now.

"Again, my King, you are many steps ahead of our enemies…" Commander Testlar told King Degnal, "…How did you know, my King?"

King Degnal did not like being questioned by subordinates in this way. Suddenly, he felt that his authority was being challenged.

"My knowledge of these occurrences is not to be questioned!" King Degnal shouted at his trusted servant.

Commander Testlar bowed low before his King. He had not meant to offend him in any way and worried that he might have overstepped his bounds this time. Though their relationship was closer than that of King, servant, this subject matter seemed to test the limitations.

"My apologies, my King," Commander Testlar said obediently.

"You may rise…" King Degnal told Commander Testlar, and then abruptly, "…That will be all."

Commander Testlar wasn't expecting such a blunt dismissal. He backed out of the chamber without lifting his head the entire way. All the while, he wondered what he did exactly to offend his King. Of late, he worried that his services would soon not be needed just like that of the late Advisor Burton.

CHAPTER 16. As Commander Testlar made his swift exit from the Chamber of Agreement, Princess Asha and her entourage stormed in right pass him.

"King Father!" Princess Asha screamed halting Commander Testlar in his tracks.

Princess Asha threw herself onto the floor before her father and sobbed uncontrollably.

"My daughter, rise…" King Degnal commanded, "…Rise!"

Princess Asha was helped to her feet by Kena and her handmaids.

"My daughter, what on earth is the matter?" King Degnal asked.

Princess Asha could barely speak through her tears.

"It's…it's…oh, my Father King…it's Oban…" Princess Asha sobbed.

King Degnal jumped out of his seat and stood to his feet.

"What about my son?" King Degnal barked.

Princess Asha was taken aback by her father's tone. Suddenly he seemed less warm and kind and much more aggressive and angry. Princess Asha stopped crying momentarily and studied her father carefully.

"SPEAK!" he roared.

No one moved as King Degnal stood rigidly towering over his daughter demanding she answer his question. Commander Testlar, who was already several steps down the long hallway, ran back and now patiently waited at the door in case his King needed his assistance. He was accompanied by twenty guards. All present stood at attention as Princess Asha replied.

"My Father…King…" Princess Asha began, but was cut off.

"Girl!" shouted King Degnal.

"Prince Oban…" Princess Asha said.

"Yes!" King Degnal screamed, "…What about my son?"

"He has been taken, my Father King," Princess Asha answered tearfully.

"NOOOOOOoooooooooooooo!" King Degnal shrieked.

END OF PART I

Adventures of a Thought Thief
Part II
A Calling to Courage - the challenge
Written by Beverly A. Burchett

CHAPTER 1. Princess Asha had to be carried to her chamber that evening. Naturally, she was too distraught over her brother's abduction to walk. The timing of her collapse occurred directly after she was rigorously questioned by her father, King Degnal about her own mysterious kidnapping.

"I demand that you tell me immediately the names of the conspirators who whisked you away so many moons ago from my kingdom!" King Degnal shouted at her.

All King Degnal received from her that evening was him witnessing Princess Asha collapsing to the floor. The palace Khemit, Elimu, was summoned instantaneously, and King Degnal angrily retreated to his throne, thoroughly unsatisfied. King Degnal knew now that he should have insisted his daughter permit him to seek revenge on her kidnapers after her abduction. Instead, he let her talk him out of it, saying that she was drugged and couldn't remember clearly. He regretted that moment of weakness. His daughter's safe return impeded his kingly duties. Had he pursued her captors then, they would not have even thought to take his son.

Elimu quickly arrived at Princess Asha's chamber and prepared and administered a strong potion for her, his special sleep-inducing tea of passion flower and chamomile.

Asha sipped the brew and thereupon began to doze off in her chair by the fire. Kena was so worried over her mistress, she would not leave her side, but lowered herself down at Asha's feet. Meanwhile, Elimu collected his remedies and exited having accomplished his task.

Once the Khemit was gone and all was quiet in the palace hallway surrounding Asha's chamber, the Princess suddenly bolted upright in her seat. Kena was so startled, she nearly yelled out. But Asha swiftly placed her finger across her lips and gestured that Kena not make a sound. Kena caught on quickly, and raced over to the door to make sure it was securely latched. When she returned to Asha's side, the two silently giggled uncontrollably.

"My, my Mistress, you are a clever one…" Kena whispered "…How did you manage the brew?"

"I spit it back in the cup, of course," Princess Asha

informed her.

"Ah…" Kena replied with a smile.

Kena realized that she should have known. Princess Asha had become somewhat of an expert at hiding her pregnancy in plain sight. When Princess Asha experienced her morning sicknesses, Kena hardly noticed her vomiting her meal back onto the platter. Princess Asha made it seem as if she ate something that disagreed with her. And when Asha's clothing tugged against her increasingly swelling middle section, Princess Asha would stand at particular angles that showed her body in a more flattering light. With simple pleats and sashes, she managed to look every bit the young daughter of a King, and not the soon to be young mother. So far, no one suspected her of being with child except for her seamstress, Amma Khan. She knew even before anything began to show. It was clear to both Princess Asha and Kena that Amma Khan was a complete wonder and not just with fabrics and designs.

Suddenly, Kena stared at her Mistress with a stream of concern upon her face.

"What?" Princess Asha asked.

"Will this really work?" Kena asked.

"Ah, so that is the worry I see on your face…"

Princess Asha replied, "…No need. Not only will this work, it will save this Kingdom."

With a triumphant turn, Princess Asha walked over to the fire and emptied the rest of the content in her cup into it. Kena immediately jumped up to take the dirty vessel from her Mistress' hand.

"He's a peevish, selfish runt who will be missed by no one!" Princess Asha nearly screamed.

Immediately, the Degnal Guards tapped on the chamber door thinking the Princess was in distress.

"Mistress?" one of the Guards asked.

"I'm fine," Princess Asha reassured them.

Kena didn't wish to argue with her Mistress, but they had just left the King's presence and he was at least one who appeared greatly disturbed by the news of his son, Oban's disappearance. In fact, he bellowed shamelessly in agony and then demanded everyone leave his sight. Had it not been for Princess Asha fainting, he would have thrown her out too.

"I know what you are thinking, Kena…" Princess Asha said, "…Yes, my Father King will miss the little toad, but in time, in time, he shall receive a new son…a greater son…my son."

"Brilliant, Mistress," Kena exclaimed.

"It is, isn't it? Pity I didn't think of it myself..." Princess Asha agreed, "...I will have to thank the one who did as soon as our paths cross..." she said contemplatively, "...First, my Father King will fall into the same melancholy as he had during my long absence..." she said.

"He was very distressed and ran out looking for you far and wide," Kena said.

"...I believe he will do the same for his son, the dog, and..." Princess Asha smiled.

"And?" Kena asked.

"...And when he returns this time, road weary and empty handed, I shall deliver to him a prize...a new Prince for his Kingdom," Princess Asha said joyfully.

"It will warm his heart!" Kena exclaimed with glee.

"It will..." Princess Asha smiled, "...and I will be the savior for him. He will not suffer one day of shame for not having a male heir on the throne. Unlike my Queen Mother, who is too old to do so, I will provide another for him."

Princess Asha leaned back in her seat and grinned blissfully. Kena sat beneath her and began rubbing her feet. Neither could believe their good fortune of having Prince

Oban taken away. Now, with King Degnal preoccupied traipsing all over the Great Lands to find him, Princess Asha's pregnancy would assuredly continue to go unnoticed.

CHAPTER 2. Kenneth was known for its brittle cold weathers, but that was especially true at its northernmost peaks. As the Elders stood atop one of its highest mountains, their exhaled breath froze in midair. No form of animal skin could keep the bitter chill from their aging bones. None seemed to mind though as they waited anxiously for their impending fate of the spell cast by Priest Godlumthakathi. They all knew that there was a price to pay. Unfortunately, one of them would have to give up their very life to satisfy the debt.

Priest Godlumthakathi was purposely prolonging his entrance to the gathering. He had as yet to receive the Elders' selected sacrifice. So, he languidly labored below continuing to assemble the preparations. Though the Elders had vowed to let him know in plenty of time, as the sun set, they still had not made their choice.

Finally, Priest Godlumthakathi made the long trek up the mount carrying all the necessary effects for the ritual. They were few; peppermint leaves to sprinkle on the fire of the deceased remains, and a thick blade to chop off the honoree's head. Kennethians would sing a traditional dirge throughout the ceremony intended to release the deceased's spirit into the arms of the Kenneth gods. The skull, once removed of its flesh, would then be carried on the silver plate specifically reserved for the occasion. It would remain in the village center so all from near and far could pay tribute until the next new moon.

"Greetings, Priest Godlumthakathi," Elder Isoba said, as the Priest made his appearance onto the summit.

Priest Godlumthakathi nodded to all present but did not speak. Out of necessity, he was preserving his energy. He'd require every bit of it in order to perform the rites. Each incantation had to be precise so that the deceased's journey could go about smoothly into the great beyond.

The Elders gave the Priest plenty of room as he went about cleaning the altar. He took his time scrubbing it down with a mixture of water and salt. Next, he removed a monstrously sharp knife from its sheave and washed it also in the same manner. It took the Elders aback when they saw it, as it glistened in the evening light, but they remained calm. Each said a secret prayer hoping their neck would not come into contact with its edge.

After the cleansing tasks were completed, Priest Godlumthakathi would insist upon the Elder's choice. Knowing this, the Elders quickly huddled together to discuss the matter one last time.

"Has anyone anything new to add?" Elder Isoba tiredly, asking his fellow weary brothers, "...We've been up here since first light and have not made much progress."

Everyone shook their head, "no" to his question then stood silently reserved.

"It didn't even work..." Elder Nafari said, "...How can we still be responsible for a failed spell?"

All of the Elders nodded their heads in agreement. In hushed tones, they expressed their displeasure with what they determined was the Priest's ineffective magic.

"Nafari is correct..." Elder Sam told them, "...If the butcher doesn't chop the meat, he is not paid. Excuse the analogy..." he paused, "...And, if a jeweler does not set a stone, he receives no reward. And, if a baker..."

"Yes, yes, Sam..." Elder Duna interrupted, "...We are quite aware of how these transactions work."

"As I've been saying, it did not work," Elder Nafari reiterated.

All of the Elders nodded in agreement again.

"I do not wish to wrestle with the Priest, but someone must tell him that he isn't due, how did you say it, Sam, a reward," Elder Duna said.

The Elders lowered their head in thought and then one by one they began to focus their attention on Elder Isoba.

"Why me?" he asked, "Because I am the eldest of the Elders?"

"Well…" Elder Sam began.

"You are the wisest…" Elder Duna told him, "…I'm looking at you because I hope you have something in mind besides this bloody business."

"Flattery will not work…" Elder Isoba said, "…Not this time anyway."

"Are there any among us who wish to volunteer?" Elder Duna asked the group.

END OF PART II SAMPLE

- on sale now -

www.blackcurrantpress.com
www.amazon.com
www.barnesand noble.com

- Novels -

Queen Kinni

**Smart, Sexy,
Spiritual, Strong**

**Random Acts of
Kindness**

Open Doors

**Forgiveness
Handbook**

- Children's Stories -

Upside Down and Other Places

Upside Down and Other Places at Work

Upside Down and Other Places at School

About the Author

BEVERLY BURCHETT started writing early on in life short stories, plays, poems, and songs. A graduate of the famed High School of Performing Arts, Ms. Burchett has also acted in a number of national commercials as well as a few popular films, including Fame, and Joey Breaker. Most recently, she can be seen on The Last O.G. S3:E2. Her novels are as follows: Queen Kinni, Open Doors, Smart, Sexy, Spiritual, Strong, Random Acts of Kindness, a journey, and the Forgiveness Handbook. She also has a children's book series, called Upside Down and Other Places. She's a published songwriter, and member of B.M.I. with works on Jerry *Eastman's Songbook* (album), the theme song for the Annual International Men's Day Conference called *This is What It Means to be a Man*, as well as her own album entitled *Psalm Songs*.

www.ingramcontent.com/pod-product-compliance
Lightning Source LLC
Chambersburg PA
CBHW061323200626
46813CB00017B/2834